BROKEN SPELL

Fabio Bueno

Booklings Publishing

Booklings Publishing

Broken Spell

Cover Design by Martina Elise Dalton

First Printing, 2013

ISBN: 0985877944
ISBN-13: 978-0-9858779-4-1 (paperback)

To

Janaína

Chapter 1: Skye

My life is on the right track at last. That terrifies me.

I'm afraid that something beyond my control—or worse, my own choices—might ruin everything.

That's why I seek the Goddess, the one constant in my life, the only true source of solace and strength.

As I crush dead leaves with my fingers, almost finishing my prayer, my body tingles. I sense the magical energy of another Sister nearby. In the middle of secluded Aurora Park, before dawn, it can only mean a threat.

If I were a regular witch, the source of the magic flow would be undetected. But I have True Sight, a Charm that allows me to sense others of my kind from a long range. Whoever is spying on me is sure she's unnoticed.

My Charm lets me estimate how far away this Sister is. She gets closer, but stops at what she believes is a safe distance, about eighty yards to my right, atop a gentle slope. She can't sense me from there, and she believes I can't sense her either. Turning to check on the Sister would alert her. Since she's still, I'll pretend to finish my ritual, while thinking at warp speed.

It's still dark and, since she can't sense me, she must be wearing night vision goggles. Or the two candles in front of me may be giving my position away. I open my eyes, a little but see no light to my right—she's not using a flashlight.

No other source of magic is around, but that doesn't mean anything. The Sister might have brought friends. They might be surrounding me right now. Think fast, Skye.

While chanting in a low voice and performing the ritual's gestures with one hand, my other hand discreetly reaches into the front pocket of my jeans. I carry a couple of potions, Sleep and Decay, there, just in case. Just for *this* case, actually. My other pocket has my cell. I could call 911, but I'd have to explain why I feel threatened by someone I shouldn't know is there. And what I'm doing in the park before dawn, which is against the law. Lighting fires, no less.

Or I can call Drake and be much briefer.

Disguising my movements, I get the cell from my pocket and speed-dial Drake's number. I turn on the speakerphone.

A groggy voice answers. "Skye? Are you all right?"

Instead of chanting, my lips move to say, "I'm sensing another witch. Maybe Jane. Aurora Park. North Entrance, about a hundred yards down the path, right side."

"Can you talk?" His voice is alert at once.

"Yes."

"What are you doing there?"

"I'm finishing my ritual. She's not moving." I put out the candles. Dawn is almost upon us, so I still can see—and so can my stalker. "I'll collect my stuff and leave now."

"Still no movement?"

"Nope." My candles, mortar, pestle, dried leaves, and water vial are in my bag now. I search for the flasks with the potions to reassure myself. "I'm leaving now." I plug an earphone into my cell. I don't know if the sight of a phone would scare my pursuer away or force her to make a move on me. I put the cell back in my pocket for now.

"Do you want me to pick you up? I'm ready to leave home." Drake's voice in my ear calms me down.

"No, wait," I say into the tiny mic embedded in the earphone cord. I walk to the path. For the ritual, I wanted peace and loneliness. Now I yearn for people and activity around me. Joggers, someone walking a dog, even a park ranger would be welcome. "Walking to the nearest exit now."

"Find a Tully's or another coffeehouse. They're open at this hour. Is she following you?"

"Yes, but keeping her distance. I think it's okay."

His voice takes a commanding tone. "Skye, it's not okay. She might have Knowings waiting to ambush you. You cannot sense those. I'm meeting you."

I pick up my pace, yearning for daylight. I can see the trees by the side of the trail, but not much further than that. Someone could be waiting for me in the shadows.

"Drake, it'll take too long."

"I'm five minutes away. Keep talking."

The engine of Drake's car rumbles to life.

"I'm looking around. No one's here," I tell him.

"How far are you from the exit? Where are you headed?"

"The north parking lot. I'll be there in a few minutes." My Charm tells me that the Sister still follows me.

"Go there and be in sight."

I want to run. But if I do, the Sister will know something is wrong. I'm not supposed to sense someone so far away. I need to stay collected.

3

A sudden rustle of leaves startles me. I'm caught by surprise and let out a small yelp.

"What?" Drake asks. "Are you okay?"

"Yes. Don't worry. Some little animal scared me."

"Almost there."

The parking lot is ahead of me. It's empty. I make a line for the car entrance.

Drake's Volvo appears, speeding. He sees me and stops right in front of me.

"Get in," he says while opening the passenger door.

"Thanks for the ride," I say while I get in.

"Where is she?" He makes a U-turn to leave the lot.

"She stopped. Let's go."

We leave the park and my shadow behind.

"Do you still sense her?" he asks after we've driven two blocks.

"No, she stayed there." I kiss his cheek. "You rescued me. Like a knight on a white horse. Or in a brown car."

He looks at me in disbelief. "How can you joke? What were you thinking?"

"I need to do my rituals, Drake. It's part of who I am."

"And what about Night Sisters stalking you?"

"They're part of my life now too."

He frowns. "Sorry, Skye. But this is not right. Just...be more careful. I worry."

"You're the sweetest."

Drake came for me right away. His disheveled hair and his sleepy eyes are evidence that he cares. I caress his face. My fingers linger on his cheekbones while I imagine who sculpted them in such artful precision.

"All right," he says. "But we need to talk about that."

"Soon. Now take me home. I want to give you a proper thank you for rescuing me."

A grin lights up his face.

Chapter 2: Drake

Sometimes you see only what you want to see.

Skye is smiling. Her radiant face mesmerizes me. I should think of her as a witch, or maybe as the girl who saved my life a few times and turned my life upside down.

But when I look at her, I can only see my girlfriend.

Never mind that she has magical powers. I don't care that she discovered my little sister is a witch, too. I barely remember the trouble we got into during the past few weeks. She's my girl, and in this instant, that's all that matters.

"What?" she asks.

She's not even a little shaken by the incident yesterday. Maybe she thinks being chased in dark parks is part of her regular routine now.

I come out of my reverie. "Nothing. Just creepily staring at you, like boyfriends do."

She shakes her head, still smiling. "You're one weird guy. But you're *my* weird guy." Skye wraps her warm arms around my neck and pulls me toward her. The kiss makes me forget everything else in the world.

***

Skye pulls away from our kiss and giggles. "Sorry. It's freezing!"

Is it? I didn't notice. We're at one of the lookout areas of Mount

Rainier, in front of the lodge, and I couldn't care less about the soft snow dampening my hair or the other visitors frowning at us. I don't let her pull away, looping my arm around her waist and keeping her body close to mine.

She looks more striking than ever, or maybe it's just her face contrasting with the sea of white in the background. I blurt out, "You look…" but I can't find the right words.

"What?" Her bright smile might melt the snow around us.

I say what comes to mind. "Happy."

She tilts her head and looks at me with those unreal blue eyes. "I am," she says in a soft tone.

For some reason, my cheeks burn, and I contemplate diving into the snow to quell the fire inside me. As always is the case with me, though, sense prevails.

"You were not lying when you promised to take me to paradise." She points to the sign that reads "Mount Rainier – Paradise Point."

I cannot help but chuckle. "Let's go inside. You're shivering. And they might charge us with public indecency soon."

We walk side by side to the lodge's lobby. My arm is still wrapped around her waist.

I hear her delightfully raspy voice. "But a little *private* indecency is fine, isn't it?" Skye is always teasing me. No, that's not a complaint.

"It's always welcome. Tea, m'lady?" I use a mock British accent to answer her.

"If it's not a bother," she says. Of course, her real British accent crushes my fake one.

"I love this accent," I say with my normal voice. "Why don't you use it?"

We cross over the threshold of the large French doors, and our faces start to thaw. Talk about a warm welcome.

"I just want to fit in." Her tone is apologetic. "It's hard. With Mum being who she is. And these." She points to her eyes.

"And the witch thing…" I say.

"You really should stop playing with the Veil." She lets go of me and plops down on a large sofa. She removes her jacket. The scar Jane left on her arm is almost gone, and the one on her temple is hardly visible.

I touch my scar by instinct. Yep, still there.

Skye notices my gesture. "Yours will go away soon, too."

"I know. I'll get the tea. We need to keep you hot," I say.

She rolls her eyes, but smiles too.

***

The line for coffee is long. My cell plays a "Hey Joe" riff. Call from Boulder.

"Drake! Sean and I are going to sneak into Redhook Brewery."

"Sorry, big man. I have plans with Skye."

He snorts on the other end. "Oh, yeah. Still in the honeymoon phase?"

Since he can't see it, I smile. "You could say that."

"Details! Come on."

The line moves. "You know I don't kiss and tell."

"Not fair. I've always told you every detail of my hookups."

"Yeah. Against my wishes."

Boulder laughs. "You enjoy this time, Drake. It might not last."

"What do you mean?" My voice is cautious.

"Getting the girl is the easy part, D-Man. The hard part is *keeping* the girl. Trust me."

My so-called friend hangs up, leaving me to mull that one over.

Chapter 3: Skye

I should have thought this through.

Drake is so sweet. I'm sorry that I involved him and Mona in my problems. My mind tries to make sense of the mess I've created. I found the Singularity, the most powerful Sister alive. But telling my coven would change her life forever: she'd be taken away from her family and put under permanent surveillance, not to mention having to look over her shoulder for Night covens intent on using or stealing her power.

I've told Connor and the covens that Brianna is the Singularity—at least while she is in a coma, she cannot deny it. And Brianna cannot try again to kill the *real* Singularity: Mona.

Would have I done the same if Mona wasn't my boyfriend's little sister? We'll never know, I guess. Their mother abandoned them when they were little kids. So maybe I felt it wasn't fair for the family to go through another separation.

But now I feel responsible for Mona. The only person unaccounted for is our biggest threat: Jane. She knows Mona's identity. Jane tried to kill me to absorb my magic. And Jane tried to do the same to Mona.

Now that psycho is on the loose, maybe scarred by the school fire. She almost certainly went back to the Night covens to tell them that Brianna is a red herring.

Meanwhile, I'm deceiving my own coven.

Drake is coming back with my tea, and I force a smile. He hands me the burning-hot cup. I blow on the liquid, the steam clouding my new glasses. Drake chuckles.

"You look steamy in those glasses," he whispers.

When my glasses clear, I turn to him and concentrate for a second. I still cannot see his aura, but I can see other people's. Most of them are here on leisure, so the light, orange-tinted halos meaning relaxation and contentment are the norm. I missed my glasses; I like being able to see auras. They're custom-made by a Sister in London. Maybe they'll be handy when we have to face the Night covens.

"What?" he asks. "You look so pensive."

I don't want to worry him, so I change the subject. "I'm glad that I decided to finish high school here in Seattle."

"We're happy to have a celebrity in school."

I playfully wag my finger at him. "No one except Priscilla and you need to know."

"Still can't believe your mother let you stay."

"Because I can do almost anything I want now that I've found the Singularity," I whisper.

"See? A celebrity. Well, a secret celebrity." His voice goes down a little. "What about after?"

"After?"

His eyes don't meet mine. "Yeah. After school? College?"

Oh. Drake means my future. *Our* future. Do we have a future?

"I haven't thought about it." My voice is as steady as I can manage.

He gives a half-hearted smile. "Come here," he says. I lean on his

10

shoulder, and he puts his arm around me. We sit as one, relaxed, while I sip my tea.

But my mind wanders. I haven't thought about that. And, now that I do, I realize I have no plan. No plan for college, for us, or for the mess with the Singularity.

I need a plan.

All of a sudden, our cozy afternoon atop Mount Rainier becomes a turmoil of worries for me. I'm not stringing Drake along. I care for him. What's wrong with enjoying the moment? Do we need to think about the future?

In any case, I must come up with clear next steps, for me, and for Mona. She's in this situation because of me.

As for Drake and me, we'll figure it out when the time comes.

***

When we drive the winding road home, I ask Drake, "Did you check the brakes?"

"Boulder did. He said they were okay."

"Boulder?"

His eyes are on the road. "He knows cars. Don't you trust him?"

"I trust him. I don't trust this." I tap the dashboard.

Drake's car is a 90s, light-brown Volvo wagon with wood panels on the sides. I'm surprised it still runs.

"Well, we're going downhill anyway," he says, shrugging.

I stare at him. Our conversation from before is still tugging at my brain.

"Remember we talked a while ago about college? You said you had no plans."

He sneaks a peek at me. "Yeah?"

"Priscilla told me you're taking pre-calc and physics."

"Yeah?"

"Sounds like a man with a plan," I say, trying to make my voice playful.

The silence is awkward, but I give him all the time he needs.

"Okay, I'll tell you. I have this idea." He focuses on the road for a few seconds, his hands grasping the wheel tighter. "I'm thinking about studying engineering." He peeks at me again, eyes a little wider.

"That's wonderful!"

His hands relax a little.

"What are your SAT scores?"

He answers in a low voice. "Good. I mean, my junior SATs were high enough that I'm not taking them again this year."

"That's brilliant, Drake! Why do you hide it?"

He checks the rearview mirror and lets a Lexus SUV pass us by. "I don't hide it. I just don't talk about it."

"But why?"

"Skye, we don't have money for college. I don't want to build up everybody's expectations. Especially mine." He smiles. "And I don't want people to see me as a nerd."

My boyfriend needs some tough love. "For a guy with a high SAT score, that's just dumb."

He narrows his eyes. "What is?"

"That you hide it. That you're not even trying to get into college when it's clear that it's something you want."

Drake blinks before asking, "How can you know?"

"Math and physics are hard. You wouldn't take them if you didn't have a desire to study further." He doesn't answer. "Can't you apply for a scholarship? I mean, even an athletic scholarship? You swim; you could try that."

His silence is unnerving. I can't take it. "So what do you say?"

"I'll think about it."

Satisfied, I turn my attention to the road. I say a silent prayer to the Goddess: I hope Boulder really knows enough about cars.

***

The mall is as empty as it gets. It's right after lunch, and Priscilla and I have the place almost to ourselves. One of the perks of having no school on a weekday.

Priscilla has already managed to unsettle the Forever 21 saleswoman—or rather, salesgirl—who dresses in an even more provocative way than Pri. While the girl goes, fuming, to the back of the store, we look at the pieces.

"This is nice," she says while examining a striped top.

"It's a cute shirt."

"No, I mean *this*." She points to me and then back at herself. "The two of us, girlying up. I've been seeing you much less since you started dating Drake."

I hadn't realized that. Well, she doesn't sound upset.

"What do you think of this?" I ask, showing her the shirt I have my eyes on.

She gives it a lightning-quick glance. "It's not you."

"Really?"

"A Pink Floyd muscle tee? Please. It's not anyone."

I thought Drake might have liked seeing me in the shirt. I put it back on the rack and continue browsing. "What about you? Your boyfriend, I mean?"

"I don't have a boyfriend," she answers without turning back.

"Of course you do. Mike, isn't it? Aren't you dating him?"

"I don't have boyfriends, Skye." She looks at me this time. "I

13

have hookups. Big difference." She approaches me, takes the denim shirt from my hands and throws it on the top of a rack. "Seriously, find some women's clothes, would you?"

"What's the difference?"

"You're picking men's clothes disguised as fashion."

"No," I say. "I mean, between a boyfriend and a hookup."

She tilts her head to the side. "What do you and Drake do?"

"We hang out. We go out for ice cream and coffee. He takes me to parks, the movies, on long drives. We have chats into the night. And yes, most of the time we're making out and stuff."

Pri smirks.

"What?" I ask.

"You just had the most idiotic smile I've ever seen."

"Wow, thank you."

She picks up a black-and-white polka dot bustier and studies it. "You are so falling for him. What do you mean exactly by 'make-out and stuff'?" Priscilla looks back at me.

"You know. We snuggle." My voice is low. My cheeks get warm.

"You 'snuggle'? Is this British slang or something?"

The salesgirl returns, and I don't want to say it aloud. I raise my eyebrows pointedly. "You know what I mean," I whisper. I look at myself in the mirror. Yep, my face is red.

Priscilla's grin is back. "I'm confused. I don't know if doing it makes you naughty or if using euphemisms for it makes you a goody two-shoes. But that's great. I'm happy for you."

I can't be offended by Priscilla. She's proved herself my friend many times over. And she knows about my previous not-so-great experiences with Connor.

"So what's the difference?" I ask again, trying to deflect the attention.

She shrugs. "Of all that you mentioned, the guy and I only…snuggle."

"Really?" I try not to sound judgmental.

"Yeah. And you know what? I like it. It's simple. It's all I need."

She turns abruptly to the salesgirl and starts talking colors.

And I'm left wondering how the two of us, so unlike each other, can be such good friends.

Chapter 4: Drake

When I arrive for breakfast, my dear little sister has already snatched the last Eggo from the freezer.

"Good morning. Practiced your rituals today already?"

"Shh, Drake. Don't break the Veil."

"The Veil? You are really into these witch lessons Skye's been giving you, huh?"

"Shut up. You don't know how hard it is to be the s-i-n-g-l-a-r-i-t-y."

After I unscramble her letters, I say, "Well, you didn't get magical powers of spelling, that's for sure. It's 'Singularity', sis. Might as well know your title."

How is it fair that my little sister is this secret Witch Queen? Mona, a girl whose only interests used to be black eyeliners, purple lipstick, and riveted mini-skirts?

She's only fifteen. Well, almost fifteen.

"What are we doing for your birthday? Dad asked me last night. I don't know if you're in the mood to celebrate." I scratch my head. "I mean, after the earthquake and all the magic stuff."

She pours coffee into her milk, taking her time. Then she says, "You're right. I'm not in the mood. But Dad expects it."

"I think so too. We owe it to Dad after the scare we gave him."

Mona was in the hospital after the earthquake. The earthquake that *she* created, by the way. Unwittingly, but still. This all happened while Dad was in Vegas, leaving us alone for the first time ever. He feels guilty as hell. And he doesn't even know about Mona being kidnapped.

Or about her magical powers.

"What would he like?" Mona asks.

"Why don't we go to a fancy restaurant? Not too expensive, so you can bring all your friends."

She looks away. "*All* my friends? You mean, Pain."

I bite my lip. "Well, you have Skye now. And me."

She raises her eyes. "That would work." Then she adds in a hurry, "Okay, gotta go. I'm meeting Pain on Capitol Hill. Then we have to study for tomorrow's test."

"No rest for the wicked, huh?"

She snorts and throws a half-eaten piece of Eggo at me. I dodge it, and it lands on the counter. I scoop it up and shove it in my mouth.

"Disgusting," she mumbles.

***

Skye comes to visit me. We make out in my room, like we've been doing for the past days, the past hours—every chance we get. It never gets old.

With my arms around Skye, I pull her even closer, and we roll on the bed, just kissing while time and worries melt away. I wish this moment would never end.

But it does, and we stay lying down, side by side, looking into each other's eyes.

"We have to talk," she whispers.

A while ago, I'd tense up just hearing these dreaded words. But now I'm confident enough that I answer in a relaxed way. "About what?"

"Your mother."

How about that for a cold shower? I squint. "What? Why?"

Her hand reaches for my face, and she caresses my cheek with her fingertips. "We need to know more about her to help Mona."

"Do you think my mother could be a witch too?" Questions like this have become normal in our recent conversations.

"It's a possibility. Do you mind talking about her?"

Still lying down, I shrug. "It's not that I mind talking about her; it's just there's not much to tell. She left us when I was little. That's about it." It's not true. I do mind talking about her. But not with Skye.

Her eyes never leave mine. "Do you have an address? A phone number? Pictures?"

"No, nothing. I have only a few memories." The warmth of Skye's hands against my skin puts me at ease.

"Bad memories?"

"Good ones. From all that I remember, she was a good mother. Before, you know, *abandoning* us." My voice cracks a little.

Skye raises herself on one elbow and hugs me, resting her head on my shoulder. "We'll talk about her later. Now I just want to stay here with you."

For many reasons, I happily agree.

Chapter 5: Skye

The restaurant is fancy, but not obnoxiously expensive. Mr. Hunter has chosen well. Except for one thing.

"Are you sure, Skye? Just a salad?" Mr. Hunter asks.

"I'm a vegetarian…"

"Oh," he says. "Not a great idea coming to a steakhouse, then. You should've told me, buddy."

Drake says, "It'd be easier to warn you if you didn't want to make it a surprise."

Mr. Hunter drove us all here. He looks dapper and much younger in the blue suit with his hair groomed.

"Mr. Hunter—"

"It's Ben, Skye. No need to make me feel older than I am."

"Nice suit, Ben."

His face lights up and he looks down to his chest, as if seeing the suit for the first time. "Thank you, Skye. It's new. I got it for the convention."

Drake is wearing somewhat formal attire. Well, formal for him: a blue and white pinstriped dress shirt. Pain and Mona are dressed in *their* version of formal.

Mona looks stunning in a black goth dress, with a laced halter strap and a draped skirt. Her long black gloves are lying on the table.

The Allure makes her even more gorgeous.

Pain's dark green gown is beautiful, but she's too tall for it. She looks uncomfortable. And she should've eased up on the makeup, especially the green eye shadow. Her hair is a miracle of styling, looking classy even with one side almost shaved.

"I love seeing you all dressed up, Mona," I say.

"Thanks. These are our sophomore dance dresses. They're so expensive, so it's nice to use them another time. Also, we need to break in these damn heels."

"Do you have dates for the dance?" I ask.

Drake groans.

"We're both going stag. Well, not really, since we're going together." Pain smiles at Mona, the first time I've seen Pain not tense. Few Knowings are as devoted as Pain.

"Excuse me for a moment. Need to wash my hands," Mr. Hunter says abruptly and leaves. He's a bad actor. I know he'll be talking to the staff about the cake he dropped off earlier in the day. Judging by Mona's smirk, she knows what's going on.

We're in a corner booth away from the other patrons, so I take the chance to talk about the Veil. "Are you drinking your Protection potions, Mona?"

She's getting the hang of it. Her eyes scan the surroundings. Good job. "I don't miss a day."

Pain taps Mona's hand affectionately and whispers, "I call her every morning to remind her, Skye. Not that she needs it." Pain's voice is slightly high and sweet. It doesn't fit her tall figure or her harsh expression. At all.

Drake asks, "Are you sure going to the dance is a good idea? With Jane out there?"

"We're taking precautions. We'll share a limo with some girls, and Skye gave us a few potion vials to use in an emergency."

"I want to be there. I'll be outside, making sure you're safe," I say.

Pain and Mona look at each other. Pain nods.

"Okay," Mona says. "A chaperone of sorts."

Mr. Hunter is back. "What are you guys talking about?"

"The dance, Dad," Mona says. "What else?"

***

Ten days later, Drake and I are in his car, parked outside Mona's school gym. It's the night of her dance, and the Volvo wagon stands out in the sea of luxury cars and limos.

"Do you sense any witches?" he asks me.

"No, nothing. We need to keep an eye out for Knowings, but Mona is safe tonight. She has the potions and the cell."

"And Pain."

"Her too."

Most students are already inside. The parking lot is quiet, except for a few parents and relatives waiting, like us.

"You're enjoying this bodyguard stuff, aren't you?" I ask him.

"As long as absolutely nothing happens to her." He looks at me with a glint in his eye.

"What?"

Drake says, "Well, since we're at the dance, we should probably make out."

"Should we?"

"Definitely. It's a tradition."

"Oh, I wouldn't want to mess with tradition. I'm a very traditional girl."

"I know you are," he whispers before kissing me.

A wave of warmth washes over me. Every time a few hours pass between our encounters, I forget how good it feels.

Only this time, an annoying tingling accompanies it. I break off the kiss and say, "I sense someone."

His eyes are trained on me. "Where?"

"At the dance," I tell him while opening the car door.

He follows me, not bothering to lock the car.

We rush to the gym. I take out my cell and call Mona. It goes to voice mail. We reach the entrance.

A smiling middle-aged woman wearing large glasses addresses us. "Invitations, please."

Drake points inside. "We're chaperoning my sister. I need to get a message to her. She's not answering her phone."

"Sure, sweetie. Go right in."

Inside, it's hard to see. The dim lights and the crowd hide Mona. And whoever is stalking her.

"We're close. She should be sensing me now. To our left." I tip my chin to the other side of the gym.

Drake gives me his keys. "Go after her. You have the radar thing. I'll find Mona."

I nod and try to traverse the sea of partygoers. They're playing an old slow dance number, and all the couples are on the floor.

The tingling sensation is diminishing a bit. The Sister is getting away.

Disregarding any pretense of politeness, I bump and push through the crowd. A few groans and complaints are hurled my way, but for the most part the dancers are too engrossed in their moment to protest. I still cannot see who I'm after.

An alarm sounds off in the direction I'm going. A back exit door was opened. The noise is muffled by the music. Now the siren and the energy signature point to the same place.

I arrive just as a teacher is about to close the door.

"Excuse me," I say, pushing through the opened door.

"Hey," he yells.

I'm back at the parking lot. I see a silhouette—a woman—getting into a silver Focus in a hurry. That's her. In a split second, I calculate in my head the best course of action. She'll be gone before I reach her car. Better to get the Volvo and use my True Sight to guide me.

It takes too long to get to the car. The tingling is faint now. She's left the lot. I turn on the engine and take off after her.

Drake's car takes forever to accelerate. A couple of blocks away from the school, the energy vanishes. I've lost her.

I pull over, call Drake, and tell him the news.

"I'm here with Mona and Pain. No strangers approached them, and they didn't see anything unusual."

"Drake, I got a look at the Sister. It wasn't Jane."

"Damn! It means Jane told someone else!"

"Yes," I say. "The Night Sisters must know about Mona."

Chapter 6: Drake

Worries swirl inside my head. I thought Skye would occupy my mind during all my waking moments (and a few sleeping moments too; I can't lie), but other issues are creeping inside my noggin.

College is still a distant dream. Fremont High won't offer the advanced courses that I was taking at Greenwood. Planning is not my thing. Just thinking about the future is unsettling. Now that I finally have a present with Skye, am I supposed to worry about the future? It seems a waste of time.

This is annoying, all right, but not life or death. My main concern is, of course, Mona's well-being. She needs to be safe. For that, I need to know more about the witch stuff.

Skye wakes me from my daydream. "Why are you so serious?"

"Just thinking." I kick a pebble out of the trail path. It goes tumbling and rolling until it falls into Lake Washington. The gray of the lake is darker than the gray of the clouds today.

"About?"

"Why exactly you decided not to tell the covens about Mona?"

She adjusts her ski cap. "Oh, wow. Are we brooding today or what?"

"If you don't want to go there—"

"No, it's not that." She lets go of my hand and grabs my forearm with gentleness. "It's just hard to describe. But you deserve the full explanation." She takes her time, but at last, she whispers, "Okay, please don't hate me for what I'm about to tell you."

"Is it that serious?" I glance at her face. She looks helpless.

She lets out a little groan. A *cute* groan. "No. I don't know. Just hear me out. When I hid Mona, it was a snap decision. I mean, I made up my mind while we were dragging you and Brianna away from the school fire."

The silence comes back. "How did you decide?"

"To understand it, you need to see it with my eyes. If we're born Sisters, then that's what we will be our whole lives. It's not only part of who we are, it's *who* we are, you see? We start to learn stuff at an early age, so we're prepared when Daybreak comes. Then the real training begins. I've seen girls older than me, and all they do, all they think about, is the Craft."

"But still, you can do magic."

"Sure. Don't get me wrong. It's great. Amazing, really. Being a witch is the greatest experience and totally worth the countless hours of training. But Mona wouldn't be your regular witch—"

"As regular as a witch can be…"

She bumps her shoulder against mine. "Silly. But a good point," she concedes.

"How can they get to Mona? If she's in danger, she can always start a fire or a blaze."

"Not without breaking the Veil, she can't. Then every coven on Earth will be after her again. And what if they—I don't know—knock her out and steal her powers before she wakes up?"

I feel a bitter taste in my mouth. "So Mona would be doing what? Training her whole life? Incarcerated in a monastery or something?"

Skye looks at me with pleading eyes. "That's where the 'don't hate me' part comes into play. I don't know."

"You don't know?"

"Not for sure. I can make an educated guess. Mona would be taken from your family. She'd have to live far away, only surrounded by Sisters and trustworthy Knowings."

"Wouldn't that be her choice? They wouldn't make her a prisoner, right?"

She stops, making me halt too. "No. Any other Sister, maybe. But not Mona. She hasn't been raised as a Sister. Her power is so unfathomable that they can't take that risk. If Mona is exposed, we all are. The covens just can't hope for the best and let her be free. They must ensure the Singularity will never break the Veil."

We see a cyclist and step out of the way, onto the grass. I look around, confused, as if the real world is the strange one.

"And what would they do?"

"That's what concerns me the most, Drake. They would do anything. We've heard stories about how rebellious Sisters were kept in check with potions and spells. To protect the Veil."

"I thought you were the good guys."

Her expression hardens. "We are. But we can't be passive when someone threatens our existence. Even if the threat comes from inside our own circles."

The chilly wind strikes my face. On the lake, a couple of seagulls are playing tag.

"So do you hate me?" Skye asks. Her voice is raspier than before.

I lean over and kiss her. She hugs me tight.

Her face is close to mine when I whisper, "I could never hate you. I need to think about this more. You may have made the right decision, after all."

"The truth is, it should be your decision too. And your Dad's. And Mona's most of all, of course."

We hold hands and resume our walk.

Something tugs at my brain. I ask her, "What makes you think Mona is in better hands now? We know nothing. She can do magic and post it on YouTube, for all we know, and we wouldn't be able to stop her. Why would she listen to us?"

"Because you're family. And I'm her friend. Mona listens to us. She trusts us. And we trust her."

"Does that make a difference?"

"Maybe that's the only difference that matters."

***

When I imagined having a steady girlfriend, I always listed the perks. We'd date and make out and do nothing and everything. It didn't cross my mind that there would be much more than that. Not negative things. Just unexpected things.

Skye is a person, not a figment of my imagination or an idealized poster girl. She has the average number of problems of a regular girl, plus the considerations of being the daughter of a famed movie star. Oh, and a witch. Not a regular witch—a celebrity witch, since she found the Singularity.

There's also the annoying fact that her ex, Connor, is a witch dude as well. I try to be cool about it, I really do, but it's…complicated. I want to be the understanding boyfriend, not the psychotically jealous one, but in the end I feel like a mix of both.

She told me that he called and asked to meet her. His request did not sit well with me.

At home, alone, I try to wrap my head around it. I look around the kitchen, trying to figure out something useful to do. Even homework would be fine, but my school was razed by the fire. That's how nervous I am: I miss school.

Sometimes it feels like a dark cloud follows me everywhere. Then I realize I live in Seattle.

I open the fridge, looking for a Coke, but I find only green tea and a Red Bull. Energy drink it is.

Bad choice. After a few minutes, I get even antsier. I resist the urge to call her.

It's not that I'm concerned that something could happen. I trust Skye. I don't trust her ex, especially with all those Fancy Me potions flying around. He's a player. I can tell. I've been friends with Boulder and Sean long enough.

The front door opens, and Mona comes in.

"In here," I shout.

She joins me in the kitchen. "You look terrible. Are you drinking? Alone?"

"Where have you been, Mona?"

"Having a life. Definitely not being miserable by myself. And where's Skye?"

"I don't know. She might even be meeting her ex—"

"She dumped you again? Is that why you're drinking?"

I raise the can with the label toward her. "It's an energy drink, sis. Skye is doing witch stuff, I guess." I empty the can and smash it on the table.

Mona is startled.

"Sorry," I say. "I just wish all the witches were girls."

Mona squints at me. "You're imagining them dancing naked in the woods, aren't you?"

In spite of myself, I snort. "No, no! Well, I am *now*."

"Have fun with the thought. Now, I'll go do homework. Some of us have school tomorrow."

"Yeah. Thanks for setting my school on fire, by the way."

She smirks. "When do your classes start?"

"They say Fremont will be ready for us on Monday."

"Are you all going there?"

"Yes. I don't know how Priscilla did it, but her father made the district put us all in the same school."

"Hey, speaking of fathers: where's ours?"

"Still working."

Mona starts to climb the stairs. "Some things never change."

Chapter 7: Skye

One of the best things about not having school is spending the morning with your hot boyfriend. His sister is in school; his father, at work. We have the house to ourselves. But we stay in the bedroom.

For once, Seattle's weather is welcoming. The trickle of raindrops on the roof is relaxing. My phone plays an endless Maroon 5 playlist at such a low volume that we can't hear the lyrics. Not that we're paying any attention to the sounds around us.

Drake and I have lost our shirts, and we're under the sheets. From time to time, we stop to rest. I'm in no hurry. We have all the time in the world.

During one of these breaks, he props himself on one elbow while I lie down by his side, my eyes closed. He touches the tattoo on my hips, lingering there for a while. I catch my breath, but his hand moves to caress the fading scar on my arm, then the one on my temple. I feel his fingertip tracing my forehead, my eyebrows, the bridge of my nose, my cheekbones. His slightest touch sets my body on fire.

Only the natural light of a dark gray day enters the room through the rain-stricken windows. The softness of the dim light allows me to be less shy. It's cold outside, but in here, the heat increases.

I roll onto his chest and kiss his neck softly. It's his turn to keep his eyes shut. My pale skin contrasts with his darker complexion. His arms embrace me in a loose grip while my lips make their way to his broad swimmer's shoulders. I dare to give him soft bites. I'm not sure what he likes, but until he tells me to stop, I'll enjoy myself. My kisses spread to his toned upper body. His chest goes up and down as he takes deep breaths. My hands cannot stop touching his hardened abs.

The fragrance of lavender and aloe body wash entices me. Drake was taking a shower when I let myself in this morning. I thought hard about being *very* forward then, but I decided for the slow approach. I'm glad I did. Now I can't help it: I'm giving in to my impulses.

"Do you like it?" I whisper.

"I do." His response is almost inaudible.

"Would you like to do the same to me?"

He smiles and opens his eyes. I lie back and pull him toward me.

Drake does as requested and kisses me, starting with the side of my neck. It tickles me at first, but before long, goose bumps spread over my skin. His kisses are firmer, stronger. His warm breath stirs me. When he reaches my shoulder, he slides my bra straps down with gentleness. I know the smallest movement might make him hesitate, so I stay still. But he just leaves the bra, untouched, partially covering me, and takes his lips down to my belly. My back arches; my muscles tighten. Soon I loosen up and let out an involuntary moan. He knows me; he knows how to drive me crazy.

"Enjoying it?" he asks in a low tone.

"Very much." My eyes are still shut. I giggle.

"What?"

"You're using your bedroom voice," I say.

"I like to be accurate, you know, location-wise. I'll shut up now."

His lips resume their exploration. He kisses the side of my tummy and comes back to the region he skipped. His mouth touches the exposed top of my chest.

I melt.

"Wait…" I tell him.

He pulls back slowly. I look at him. He's still smiling.

"Excuse me a little bit," I say, squeezing from under him and leaving the bed.

Drake's face works hard to hide his disappointment. But he has no reason to.

Still gazing at him, I walk to the bedroom door and lock it. "Just in case," I say, using *my* bedroom voice.

His full smile returns. His sinuous, sculpted torso beckons.

I go back to him.

Chapter 8: Drake

Seattle's maddening weather has never been sweeter. I had never noticed how much the gray clouds look like classic marble sculptures. I decide to leave the car at home and walk.

The cold breeze lashing at my face makes me feel alive. The constant drizzle of the rain cleanses me and energizes me for a new day. I walk to the pool with light steps, as if I'm floating above the ground. Life is good.

When I arrive at Greenwood, I cast a glance to the main building. They have almost finished removing the debris and cleaning the area. The reconstruction will take some time. I feel a twinge of guilt before remembering it couldn't have been avoided. It was an accident, and nobody got hurt. Well, except Brianna and me. And we ended up better than expected. You know, alive and all.

Soon the thought leaves my head, and I open the door to the pool building across the street from the school. The pool hasn't been damaged, and it's still open for students.

Splashing sounds and chattering startles me. I enter the pool and find the swim team practicing.

I usually pick a time when the pool is deserted, but today I forgot to check. I just wanted to swim.

A lane is reserved for laps for the public. I'll use that one.

But Coach Summers sees me before I head to the locker room. "Hey, Mr. Hunter! The Black Swan himself. Did you finally decide to join the team?" He gestures to the gang of Speedo-clad, goggle-wearing guys and girls racing in the water.

I smile at him. For some reason, the talk I had with Skye is imprinted in my mind. College. Maybe a swim scholarship.

"May I?"

Skye is right. What's the big deal? Why can't I swim with folks? I can do my thing and be eligible for a scholarship if my times are good enough. Maybe things will break my way.

"Come on, don't be sarcastic with an old man. It's disrespectful."

"No, I mean it. May I practice with the team?"

Coach Summers stops and looks at me as if I'm one of the body snatchers' clones. "What are you talking about? You, the loner, want to join?"

"It's not actually a team sport, is it?" I say.

His eyes narrow. "It totally is. The events are individual, but we're a team. Always remember that."

"Okay," I say.

He doesn't say anything. He just looks at me.

"So what do you say, Coach? Come on, you've been pestering me for months to join the team. And when I finally agree, you treat me like this. Were you joking about it?"

"Are you?"

"I'm a hundred percent serious. I want to try out for the team."

A smile the size of the skyline blossoms on his face. "That's great news." He looks at me and grins like a kid. He catches himself soon, though, and his face regains its crusty expression. He barks, "What are you waiting for? Get ready and jump in! We don't have all day."

"Yes, sir." I head to the locker, but look back to sneak a peek at him. He's smiling again.

Good moods are contagious.

***

"What's up with Sean?" I ask Boulder.

Boulder is driving us to the mall. In the backseat, Sean types on a laptop. Not only Sean has given up shotgun, he's silent. And, most shocking of all, typing.

"Hey, Shakespeare, wanna tell him?" Boulder yells.

"What? I'm writing," Sean says, eyes glued to the screen.

"Sean's taking online screenwriting classes. He wants to write the next blockbuster. A Hollywood snob." Boulder shakes his head.

"Hey, be supportive, dumbass," Sean tells him.

I agree with Sean. "Yeah, Boulder, don't be a hater."

"I'm not a hater. I'm a huge disliker."

Sean raises his head. "You're going to be a character in this one, big man."

"Really?" Boulder is interested all of a sudden.

"Yeah! I'm thinking Passerby Number Two. You'll die a gruesome death."

Sean and I cackle and high-five. I've missed that. Being one of the boys.

"You sure you wanna do that, little writing man? It's on! It's *so* on."

"Where are we going?" I ask.

Boulder says, "I need a new haircut. Need to look good for the Fremont girls. Can't rely only on my chick lasso."

Chapter 9: Skye

Drake and I arrive for our first day at Fremont High. He sees Boulder's car in an isolated corner of the parking lot, drives up, and parks next to it. The bright yellow Mustang and the muted brown Volvo couldn't make for a bigger contrast.

Through the window of his car, Boulder nods in our direction. He lowers the window and motions for me to do the same. "Where's Priscilla?" he asks.

"She texted me. She's almost here."

Boulder nods again. It's weird seeing this hulking guy so nervous. It was his idea to brave the new school together.

Fremont High is the home of the Spartans. Drake told me that when Boulder played football, he caused a full-on brawl between Greenwood and the Spartans. Our old school forfeited the game and Boulder was kicked off the team. He is concerned that the Spartans may gang up on him. And his former teammates, still pissed at him for costing them a victory, most likely won't come to his rescue.

"Why do you need us?" I ask him. "Priscilla and I wouldn't do much good in a fight."

"Guys will die to impress hot girls like you. No way they want you to see them as jerks. Just stay around me, and I'll be fine."

"Are you afraid, Boulder?"

"It's not fear. It's tactics," he snarls, glaring at me.

I look past Boulder and see Priscilla sneaking in front of the car. She raises her hands and bangs on the Mustang's hood.

Boulder jumps in his seat. Priscilla laughs and walks between the two cars, approaching our windows.

"You on edge, big boy?"

He grumbles. "Just be careful with the machine."

Priscilla chuckles. "Okay, I'm here to protect you. Can we go now?"

The four of us get out of the cars and assemble. People are already staring at us.

"Don't worry," Sean says. "They're looking at your egg-yolk car, big man."

"Maybe it's Drake's stool-colored one."

"Hey!" my boyfriend protests.

Priscilla shakes her head. "Let's get this over with."

She takes point. Drake holds my hand, and we trail her. Boulder and Sean follow, trying to hide behind the group. They scrunch up a little, looking ridiculous, since they are even taller than Drake.

Boulder's "tactic" is backfiring. Priscilla looks like a model, and Boulder looks like a linebacker—which he was. Together, they practically force the Fremont students to stare at our group.

I feel a sudden tingling. Two sources of magical energy are closing in on us. I slow down and look back to the parking lot, trying to find the witches. Priscilla, Sean, and Boulder pass me by and continue their awkward march, but I don't follow them. I'm curious.

Drake stays with me and keeps silent, his hand still holding mine.

The sensation intensifies. Even knowing the general direction, it's hard for me to determine who they are. Too many students are arriving at the same time.

But a couple of them are turning their attention to me. Two girls. One of them looks familiar. Before I can place her, though, she approaches and greets me.

"Hey, it's you!" A pierced girl with dark make-up flashes me a broad smile.

I blink a few times before a name comes to me. "Greta?"

She opens her arms, moves forward, and gives me a cozy hug. With her so close to me, the sensation of my True Sight Charm becomes a faint electric shock. The other girl, a beauty with large brown eyes and curly black hair, wearing a Sailor Moon tee, stares at us with an amused smile. I can easily feel her energy too.

Greta lets me go and turns to Drake. "Hi to you, too. Boyfriend or beard?"

"Boyfriend. Name's Drake," he says.

Greta doesn't blink, but her eyebrows rise the slightest bit. She points to the anime girl. "This is Yara."

Greta's pale complexion contrasts with Yara's. It's weird seeing them together: a goth girl clad in black and a sunny Sister dressed as if it were summer.

Yara waves to us, exposing an exquisite silver mermaid tattoo on her right arm. I glance at Drake, who is staring at the tattoo. His eyes then go straight to Greta, the silver moon inked on the back of her neck partially visible to him. I tug on his hand to snap him out of it.

"Nice tats," he says, trying to disguise his indiscretion. "Same color and everything."

"Yeah," Greta says slowly, narrowing her eyes and touching the nape of her neck as if by instinct. "BFFs, you know?"

Drake nods, unconvincingly.

I turn to him. "Drake, why don't you go check on the guys? See if they're in trouble."

He looks at me, confused. "I'm sure they're fine."

I purse my lips.

"On second thought, they might need me," Drake says in a hurry. "Nice to meet you." He nods at Greta and Yara and leaves.

Yara pulls out her phone and starts texting. She does it so quickly her fingers are a blur.

"Is he a Knowing?" Greta asks.

I nod. "Hey, what are you doing here? I thought you went to Ballard."

Greta shrugs. "This is my school. I just moved temporarily to Ballard to help with the Search. After you found the Singularity, I came back here. Thanks for finding her, by the way. I hated those snobs at Ballard."

"And Yara was responsible for Fremont?"

"Uh-huh. Come on, let's go. The bell is about to ring."

Greta moves to walk and holds my hand, pulling me with her. I don't know how to react, so I just hold her hand back and walk beside her. I look back and see Yara still pounding the phone, following us with her eyes on the screen.

A commotion at the front steps of the building stops us. Boulder is at the center of the gathering. Why am I not surprised?

"Seriously? You're coming here?" A big guy is yelling at Boulder. The guy's oversized belly shows beneath his tight t-shirt. He is sweaty, his shaved head glistening even in the cold weather. A slightly smaller jock has his hand on the chest of the bigger guy, as if holding him back.

Boulder makes an apologetic gesture. "It's not like I had an option. There was a freaking earthquake."

Greta whispers to me. "That's DeMarcus. He's our center."

"Basketball?"

"Football."

Boulder continues, "Dude, I'm off the team, okay? That good enough for you? Now let's just go our separate ways."

DeMarcus points his finger at Boulder. "I don't care. Because of you, we'll be having classes there." DeMarcus's finger moves to the right of the building. Four portables sit on the football field.

"Behind the portables?" Boulder asks.

"*Inside* the portables, bro," the smaller big guy answers.

Sean laughs, and everybody looks at him. Boulder elbows him. Sean grabs his side and doubles over, letting out a grunt.

Boulder puts his hand on his forehead and says in a calm voice, "Dude, you can hate me all you want, but you can't blame me for that."

The bell rings before DeMarcus and his buddy can reply. The crowd starts to disperse. The two jocks give my friends murderous sideways glances before joining the throng. Some are going inside the building; others are going to the football field.

Drake and Priscilla emerge from the other side of the crowd and wave to us.

Greta says, "We don't have enough space for you guys. We're improvising with portables. The students—" Greta stops mid-sentence and whispers to me, her chin pointing at Priscilla. "Does she have Allure?"

"She's not a Sister," I answer.

Boulder looks around and sees us. "Come on, let's go. Everyone already hates us; no need to make the teachers our enemies too." He grabs the still bent-over Sean by the collar of his shirt and guides him to the building.

"And who is this big guy?" Greta asks again.

"A troublemaker. And a trouble magnet, too."

"Just my kind," she says, showing me a wry smile.

Chapter 10: Drake

Skye may be right: Mona is a Sister, so my mother might be one too. The problem is that my father never talks about her.

After I finish my homework, I head downstairs. Dad is watching Sportscenter. It's rare that he has a free weeknight—he usually works late. I feel bad intruding on his downtime, but I need to know.

"Hey, Dad."

He turns to me, surprised, and gestures for me to join him. "Hey, buddy."

We watch the Top Ten Plays in silence.

During the break, Dad asks, "How's the new school?"

"Different. Still adjusting."

"At least the guys are going to Fremont with you. And Skye, too?"

"Yep."

He pauses, waiting for me to expand on that. When I don't, he asks, "Is the car running well?"

"It is. It had a noise the other day, but Boulder fixed it. He said it may be something electrical. I need to check it out."

"Good."

Dad turns his attention to the TV. They're talking about a possible Mariners trade.

"I was thinking about Mom," I blurt out.

He faces me. "Yeah?" His voice carries no emotion.

"I wanted to know more about her." I look down for some reason. I hear him sigh.

"We've had this talk before, buddy. We lost her pictures in the house fire. And I told you and Mona a lot about her already."

Shifting my body to face him, I say, "Yes. I know you met her in your last year of college. You dated two years, while she was getting her nursing degree, and then married. Her family didn't show up for the wedding. I know her date of birth and that she loved chocolate ice cream."

"There you go. So?"

"So it's just facts. That's like her Wikipedia page, Dad. That's not who she was. Or is."

He looks at the TV again. "I don't know what you mean."

"Why did Mom leave, Dad?"

He clicks the remote, turning the TV off. Still not facing me, he says, "Why are you asking? Why now?"

"We've never really talked about it."

"There's not much to talk about. She left. She said she needed to do other things with her life." He does a remarkable job of keeping his voice steady.

"You must hate her."

"Not at all. If anything, I pity her."

"Pity her?"

He finally looks at me. "I get to live with you guys. I got to see you grow up. You asked me about the reason she left. I don't know. But it must have been pretty compelling for her to miss out on you and Mona." Then he stands up. "I'm exhausted. Going to bed. Good

43

night, buddy."

***

"Is that all that he said?" Skye asks.

"Yep."

School's over, but we linger in the parking lot. Most kids are already gone. It's thirty-five degrees, but the sun is out, and we endure the cold to get a little light.

"Can't you get more from him?"

"This is not my first try. The guy is a rock. And I don't want to force it. It hurts him."

She taps my hand. "It was a good idea. But if he won't talk... Is there anyone else we could ask? Your grandparents?"

"My mother's parents died before she met Dad. Maybe Dad's parents would know something. But Nana and GG hate my mother for leaving. They are even more closed up than Dad."

"GG?"

"That's Grandpa George." I recall a few awesome spring breaks we spent at Nana's.

Skye giggles.

"What?" I ask.

"You spaced out for like two minutes."

"I did not!"

"You miss them, don't you?"

"They live in Boca, and they come every year on the Fourth of July. You'd like them. Nana is super nice, and GG is a fitness freak who looks almost Dad's age. They never stop talking. I love it."

She gives me a peck on the cheek. "Maybe I'll get to know them."

Her declaration implies something I never thought about.

"I'd like that," I say.

44

Chapter 11: Skye

"It all starts with relaxation, Mona."

We have not been having much progress in our first few training sessions. Mona is a dedicated student. Her eyes are trained on me; she listens to my instructions. But it is still not working.

We're deep into Saint Edward Park's woods, on the Eastside. We deviated from the long trail that leads to the lake and found ourselves a nice little clearing away from curious ears. It wasn't necessary: the park is almost deserted, even in late afternoon. Besides, we're not doing any rituals today. The place is a former seminary. Maybe it will be conducive to peace, quietness, and meditation.

She cranes her neck, making the bones crack with dull sounds that cause goose bumps on my arms. Then she closes her eyes and winces. Her body is still, but I notice her biting her lip.

"What are you doing?" I ask.

"Trying to relax, as you said."

"You may be trying too hard?"

"I need to focus to be relaxed."

I chuckle. She looks at me, puzzled.

"The whole point of relaxing is not focusing on anything," I say. "Clear your mind. Feel the nature around us. See if you can sense the earth energies emanating from the ground. They may be faint, but they're there."

She looks at the dirt in front of her, as if trying to *see* the energy. "Sorry. I can do it when I'm with Pain."

"You can relax when you're hurting?"

It's her turn to chuckle. "No, silly. *My* Pain. My friend."

"Oh. Right. I'm not comfortable inviting her to our meetings for now. Not until you get the hang of it. Besides, you need to learn to do it by yourself."

Mona nods. She flexes her facial muscles, as if making faces. It works for her: her expression is calmer now. Or maybe she just needed a laugh.

We stay still for a while. I watch her. Her breathing is steadier; her face devoid of worries. She's got it. I close my own eyes and soon enter a state of meditation.

It's broken by a deep breath. I open my eyes to see Mona staring at me.

"I think it worked." I smile.

"It did!" She shows me her watch. "Four minutes. It's like I was passed out."

"What else did you feel?"

"Not much. Just a kind of void. But then I was dying to see how much time had passed."

"With more training, you'll notice the energy around you. Like our personal magic, but much fainter. Even I, with my True Sight, can only feel it when I'm meditating or doing a ritual."

She giggles. It's great seeing her so happy. "And when do I get to do those? With real magic?"

"In time. Don't worry." I tap her hand, reassuring her. "Now, do you know why we're doing this?"

"Relax to learn to meditate. Meditate so we can do rituals. Rituals so we can do spells and potions."

"Yes, that's the practical purpose of it. But the Craft isn't magic. The Craft is a way of life. You're learning how to attune to the energies of the world. Everything carries its own energy. We respect life and Mother Earth. You learned that when you were practicing Wicca, didn't you?"

Mona stretches while she talks. "Uh-huh. Pain and I stumbled through Wicca, but we were getting better. At first, we just read a lot, but soon we started doing some stuff."

"So you probably already created your own rituals. But now that you've had your Daybreak, you cannot do it without my supervision. Do you understand why?"

Her face gets gloomy. "Because I can release the Singularity's energy and level a city."

"Well, I don't expect anything that dramatic again. But you may release a suspiciously large amount of energy. Sisters could sense it and know something is off."

She nods, biting her lip.

"Good, Mona. For now, just practice relaxation and meditation every morning and evening. See if you can do it in your bedroom." I point to the ground. "This place is great to channel the energies, but for now we need to keep a low profile and make sure no one sees these sessions."

"Hiding."

"Just being careful, Mona. It will get better."

***

The coffeehouse I chose is way outside of Drake's usual stops. Even though he knows I'm meeting Connor, I don't want any mishaps.

I was intrigued by Connor's call asking for a meeting.

He opens the door exactly at four p.m. One of his few good qualities is his punctuality. All eyes can't help but look at him. Mostly female eyes. He notices the attention—and relishes it. He approaches my table and dares to kiss me on the cheek. I let him. It's harmless.

"How are you?" he asks.

"I'm good. You?"

He ignores my question. "You decided to stay in Seattle, then?"

"For a while."

"I like it here." He smirks, flaunting those impossibly white teeth.

"So you asked to meet." I want to get down to business soon. I don't want to give Connor time to be charming.

"Yes. It's about the Search," he says, lowering his voice. "It's a procedural thing we haven't got to yet."

"What is it?"

"The covens need to take your report. Officially, I mean. It was supposed to be done in London, but since you're staying, I can arrange for the Mother to come here."

"The Mother?"

"Yes. Elsa Dunivant. Do you know her?"

I freeze. I do know her. She's one of the coven Priestesses. And one of her Charms is Truth. She's a human lie detector.

"Oh, yeah," I say, nodding casually. "Do you think it's okay for her to be traveling? I mean, at her age?"

"She's fine. She travels all the time."

I hope Mum's acting chops have somehow been passed along to me. "Such a hassle. Is this really necessary?"

Connor arches an eyebrow. "Well, yes. It's important. Even for our historical records. It's the Singularity we're talking about. And you're the only witness. I mean, Brianna is still in a coma and Jane is gone," he says, making a waving gesture. "We only have your account, and even that was just a chat we had. We need to make it official."

I catch myself biting my lip. No reason to raise his suspicions. I say, "Sure. It makes sense. When is she coming?"

"I'll have to talk to our coven," he says. But his eyes wander. He's stalling.

"Couldn't you have told me this over the phone?"

"Do you know if they serve machiattos here?"

"Connor…"

"I wanted to see you," he blurts out.

"Connor!" I repeat, now in an admonishing tone.

He puts his hands up in front of him. "No, listen to me. I've been thinking about you. I miss you."

"You can't be serious. You broke up with me, remember? I was a silly little girl—direct quote."

"I know, I know. You're not anymore."

"Charming."

"No. I mean, I was wrong. And you proved it to me. You came here to help your coven. We'd been stuck in the Search for two years, and you found her in a few weeks. By yourself. You must admit, you've changed. Why can't I?"

"You're right. I've changed. Now I would never fall for you again." I don't understand him. It's clear that whatever we had once is gone. I thought we were both aware of that.

"Skye, please. At least consider it. I know I didn't behave well. But, come on. Haven't you ever made a mistake?"

I stand up. "I make them all the time. For example, today I agreed to come here."

While I walk to the door, I catch a glimpse of him shaking his head. He looks almost sincere.

***

"How are things, Mum?"

The connection is great. Mum is filming in some remote place in India, but she could be calling from the next house.

"We've just arrived. Everybody's so excited."

"Big cast?"

"Yes, an ensemble, including two of my old friends from the Company. But I have the juiciest part. It's the role of a lifetime, darling."

"That's great! Do you see an award in the future?"

Mum chuckles. "We don't act for awards, you know that. However, the movie is generating Oscar buzz, yes. And I wouldn't mind having another one. Mine is feeling lonely on our mantel."

I laugh. "I see."

"I mean it, Skye. It's not about the awards, but another prize means guaranteed work for the next few years, maybe a pick of screenplays. In this business, you need to be in people's minds. And I'm not getting any younger."

"You sure look young."

"Oh, aren't you the sweetest? May the Goddess hear you. All right, they're waving at me. We're going to visit one of the locations. I have to go."

"Okay, Mum. Have fun!"

"Kisses! I love you."

"I love you too."

"And I trust you," she says before hanging up.

I look at the phone, trying to guess the meaning of her parting words. That was weird. Anyway, I'm stoked for her. She has a blast when she's on location, especially places she hasn't visited yet.

I turn around, and my happy face meets Gemma's frowny one.

"Hey, Aunt Gemma. Mum sends regards."

"I know, I talked to her yesterday. Skye, I had to tell her about you sneaking around with that boy."

"Oh."

She waits for me to expand on that, but I don't know how to respond. It's my business, but I don't want to be rude.

"You understand why I had to let her know, right? When you're here, you're my charge."

"Okay… Well, she didn't mention it to me."

Gemma purses her lips. "Yes. She didn't think much of it. She said she trusted you."

That explains Mum's cryptic words. I smile involuntarily.

"This is not a license to do anything you want, you know?" Gemma says.

"It's okay. I know what I'm doing. Everything is all right."

She relaxes a bit. "I'm just looking out for you."

"Thanks. Mum trusts me. Can you do the same?" I hope it doesn't sound too harsh.

But she smiles. "Of course. Just know that I'm here for you. If you need me."

I'm so lucky. I hug her. "You're the best, Aunt Gemma."

She pinches my cheek affectionately.

It's good to know that Gemma and Mum are okay with my choices and have confidence in me. I go to my room in a state of joy.

51

A piece of paper lies on my bed. It looks like a note. It reads, "Don't freak out. Call me. We need to talk. Jane." A phone number is scribbled at the bottom of the note.

I instinctively look around the room, as if Jane might be behind the door ready to pounce. Taking a deep breath, I make my way back downstairs.

Aunt Gemma is making coffee in the kitchen. "What is it, dear?" she asks.

"We need to install a home security system. Just in case."

Chapter 12: Drake

The new school has a weird dynamic. I'm not comfortable with the workload, and even less with the students. At least my handful of friends go there. But classes are different; they don't even have pre-calc.

I thought about what Skye told me: that I could still enter college on a scholarship. Maybe it's too late for that. The mess with changing schools and having a new curriculum left the fate of some of our grades unknown. Besides, I thought I could get letters of recommendation from my Greenwood teachers, but they, like us, are spread across the school district now.

But this morning brings more pressing matters. As I had promised Skye, I go to the doctor. I suffered a concussion during the fire incident, and she insisted I have my head checked out.

Brianna, the Knowing who tried to kill my sister, is in the same hospital, in a coma.

The hospital choice was deliberate: I wanted to see what security the witches have around her.

But when we are still a few blocks away, Skye says, "I'm sensing a couple of Sisters. Slow down."

I reduce the speed.

"There! Pull over. If we get too close, they'll sense me too. See?

The woman at the outside table at Tully's? It's freezing, but there she is. The energy is coming from her."

"They're two blocks away from the hospital."

"Yes. She's probably a Night Sister. They can't come any closer because the hospital must be crawling with our Sisters. They need to observe—and sense—from a distance, so they don't alarm our side."

I go back to the street and make a left turn far away from the woman at the café. We go two blocks over. Skye identifies another witch there, somewhere on a high floor of an apartment building. We can't see her, though.

"They have a straight line of sight to the hospital from here. They might have a telescope pointed to the parking lot. And I bet that if we search around the hospital, we'll find more Night witches around."

We finally arrive at the hospital. Skye doesn't go inside for my consultation. She waits in the car. She doesn't want her magical signature to be picked up by the witches doing the surveillance. A witch—any witch—getting too close would sound alarms. And Skye and I want to keep a low profile.

When I get back to the car, she is anxious. "How are you?"

"I'm fine." I explain to her the exams the doctor did. I've got a clean bill of health.

I get a long kiss as a reward. Skye waits a bit before asking, "And Brianna?"

"I'm still mad at her, Skye, but you don't need to walk on eggshells. I'm a big boy. I went to her floor. I saw four people with earpieces, looking very much like bodyguards or FBI agents. Two women close to the elevator, another woman by the stairs, and a guy sitting in the ICU waiting area. And one more woman in the lobby."

"I felt four signatures from here. The one in the lobby and two other people in one of the upper floors are witches. And one somewhere from below."

It makes sense. "They may have someone staking out the garage. They need to cover all entrances."

"I'm pretty sure one of the people generating a signature on the high floor is a doctor," she says.

"A witch doctor?" I smirk.

She slaps my leg playfully. "Some Sisters with a Healing Charm decide to become doctors. They need one of them to keep an eye on her medical condition. They may have been using Healing potions to help her recover."

"This is bad news."

"It is. As long as Brianna is out cold, they have no way of knowing that she's not the real Singularity. Even if she wakes up, we'd be somewhat safe."

I turn on the ignition. My brain needs coffee. As I maneuver out of the parking lot, I ask, "Couldn't they use a Truth potion on her when she wakes up?"

"They could, but they won't: they know the Singularity has all those natural magical shields and that a potion may not work on her. But the covens won't wait forever. They will have Sisters with Intellect Charm trying to figure it out. Sooner or later, they'll conclude that Brianna is not the Singularity."

"What do we do then?"

Skye just shakes her head. "We'll figure it out when the time comes."

***

After I'm properly caffeinated, I drive her to Aunt Gemma's

house. All the worries about Brianna and Mona and Singularities are on the back burner for now. "Up for a movie tonight? We could see the new James Bond. You know, in case you're homesick."

"You are silly. Oh, I forgot to tell you. The girls asked me to go out with them tonight."

"The girls?"

"Greta and Yara."

"The 'Weird Sisters' are 'the girls' now?"

"Please don't call them that."

"What about Priscilla? Isn't she one of 'the girls'?"

"Priscilla is going out with her new boyfriend. I didn't even tell her."

I point to me. "Hey. New boyfriend here, too. Don't I get to go out with my new girlfriend?" I point to her.

"Come on, it was nice of them to ask me. I'm new to school. It's good to be in touch with my Sisters. Why don't you go to the movies by yourself?"

I give her a 'seriously?' look. "I'll just hang out with my two best friends: Xbox and pizza."

"What about Sean and Boulder?"

"It's no use. They're 'hunting' tonight. You don't want me with them."

We arrive at Aunt Gemma's. Skye leans over and whispers, "Come here. I'll give a little something to keep you warm tonight."

This new boyfriend stops complaining.

***

When I'm getting my pizza from the oven, I hear a car in our driveway. Muffled voices chatter happily. I go to the window to see what's going on. Mona is waving goodbye to two dudes in an old, light-blue Civic. The car leaves, and Mona saunters to the front door.

I go back to find a pizza cutter and start cutting slices. The front door opens.

"Hey, Mona. Pizza?"

She drops her purse on the sofa and joins me in the kitchen. "Sure. I'm starving."

"Got a ride home, huh?"

"Uh-huh." She grabs a diet green tea bottle from the fridge.

"Do I know those guys?"

"How do you know they were guys? Are you spying on me?"

"You've never had guys taking you home before." I hand her a plate with a slice of pizza, but she doesn't take it from me.

Instead, she keeps staring at me. "Are you a big brother now? Or *the* Big Brother?" She does a booming voice while making her eyes wide.

"It's just that now you're, you know…beautiful."

"Thank you. You don't need to say it in such an 'eew' voice, though."

I put the plate, still untouched, on the kitchen counter. "You know what I mean. Guys will be after you. Not with the best of intentions."

"You should know. You lock the door when you're with Skye. Maybe someone should be concerned about her."

"Ha-ha. It's not the same."

"Is that what's troubling you? Not me, let's say, destroying the whole city by accident, but guys giving me a ride?"

"I can be worried about both. I can multitask."

Mona drinks from the bottle of tea, still sizing me up. "For your information, Drake, I'm not only 'beautiful' now. I'm hot. I know.

I've been told. I'm a size 14 hottie now. Do you know how long I've waited to hear that? Do you have any idea what this means to me?"

That's unexpected. "I clearly don't."

She gets another slice of pizza, puts it on her plate, and says, "You actually do. Think about it. How did you feel when Skye started to notice you?"

Okay, she has a point.

Mona continues, "I can take care of myself, Drake. I'm a big girl now. A big, *hot* girl. And I'm a witch too. That should count for something."

She turns on her heel and goes upstairs to have her dinner.

Chapter 13: Skye

We stop in front of the nightclub. Yara lights up a cigarette, which is odd, since I've never seen her smoking. Then, still holding the cigarette between her fingers, she applies lipstick, a brand I don't recognize. We approach the bouncer, a scary-looking, large man who stands god-like behind the rope. Yara doesn't even look at the line and goes directly to him. Greta and I follow her.

My new friends' magical energy so close to me is disturbing. I haven't had this nonstop tingling since I left London and Mum. It's hard to get used to the intense sensation.

The bouncer measures up the three of us. We clearly look underage. However, Yara gets close to him, takes a deep drag, and blows the smoke right in his face. The guy in front of the line shudders. I do too. The bouncer can crush Yara with his pinkie. But before the man has a chance to react, she shows him her fake ID.

"I don't need to show ID. I'm twenty-one. I come here all the time."

The bouncer stares at her glassily through the smoke. He says in a deep voice. "You don't need to show ID. You're twenty-one. You come here all the time."

"And my friends too." She glances at the rope between them.

"And your friends too," the man parrots. He unclips the rope and motions the three of us in.

Greta nudges me in the back, and in we go. We're almost at the threshold of the door when his voice booms. "Hey!"

Yara turns back and says in a petulant voice, "What?"

He blinks a few times, apparently confused. "No smoking inside," he says in a tame tone.

Yara smirks, throws the cigarette on the floor, and stomps on it. Then she walks rapidly toward the bouncer again.

"What is she doing?" I whisper.

She stands again before him and, with her index finger, gestures him to come closer. When he does, she kisses him on the lips, mouth closed, no tongue, for a couple of seconds. She pulls away and smiles. He has a puzzled look on his face. He says nothing, though, and proceeds to talk to the man in front of the line as if nothing had happened.

Yara walks to us, a victory smile on her lips.

"What was that?" I ask Greta as we enter the club.

"I told you, she's a master of potion mixing," Greta says in my ear. "She can mix it up. She can make cigarettes, lipsticks, creams, perfumes, nail polish. Very handy, if you ask me."

I just shake my head while we enter the temple of deafness.

***

The girls go chat with a couple of guys. I lean on one of the columns and try to absorb the vibe of the place. The adjustment to the loud music and blinding lights is swift. Soon, a boy approaches me. He's a little older than me, muscular and tanned; he looks like a GQ cover model. And he uses a lot of product on his hair. "I saw you dancing. I'm Liam," he says.

"I have a boyfriend," I say.

He smiles. "Me too."

Okay, this can't be a pick-up line. At least he's not flirting. I relax a little.

He leans over. "You have a slight accent. Where is it from?" He smells good.

"London." I'm surprised he can hear the accent, especially with all the noise.

"Do you want to dance?"

"I can't dance to save my life."

"I'll teach you. Come on."

I see no harm. He holds my hand with such gentleness. His orientation is not a line. It's evident when he dances. He shakes his hips with joy and abandonment. It's contagious. Soon I'm joining him, awkwardly. He's all smiles, but he doesn't laugh.

He gets close. "Not bad! You may need some lubricant for your rusty joints. Can I get you a drink? I'm getting a pear martini."

Not a bad idea. "A Buck's Fizz for me."

"A what?"

"The bartender will know."

"Okay. Don't run away, sweetie. I *will* chase you," he says with a mock stern tone.

I just stay there, looking like a dork. Without him to copy, I just fling my arms back and forth. It's like I'm trying to take flight. But I like the idea of dancing, of letting yourself go a little. And I don't care what the other people on the dance floor think.

The electronic music finally conquers me. I'm enjoying it. The energy signatures of Yara and Greta are fainter now. They're still around, but not so close.

Liam comes back with a martini and something that's definitely *not* a Buck's Fizz.

"The guy had no idea what a Fizz was. He made you a cosmo." He hands me a pinkish drink.

Delicious. We step off of the dance floor for a while.

"Having fun? Where's your boyfriend?"

"He doesn't like to dance."

Liam scoffs. "Mine neither. Their loss." We raise our cups and toast.

He leans over to talk in my ear. "Listen, my friend got us into the VIP lounge today. Wanna join us?"

"Sorry, I'm here with my friends." I expect him to invite all of us over, but he doesn't. It's all right by me; I don't want to impose on a guy I just met.

Soon we're back dancing, and I'm clearly less inhibited after the drink.

Liam approves my moves. "You're getting it."

I let the moment take over. The thumping music, the drink, Liam's niceness. The people's energy feeds my own. My body wants to dance. I feel smooth.

The magical energy coming close to me almost goes unnoticed. I open my eyes suddenly, looking to the upper floor right above Liam.

"What?" he asks, turning to look in that direction.

The energy fades. I look around and see Greta and Yara dancing with some guys on the opposite side. It wasn't the girls' signatures.

"Excuse me," I tell Liam. "I need to talk to my friends."

Liam nods, a little concerned.

Making my way to Greta, I try to clear my head. Am I overreacting? There are other Sisters in Seattle, after all.

Greta sees me approaching and comes to talk. "Hey! You

disappeared."

"Making friends. Did you sense another Sister?"

She shakes her head. "Why? Anything wrong?"

"No, no."

Yara grabs my hand and makes me dance with their group for a while. When I try to get back to Liam, he tells me his boyfriend called. He's leaving. We exchange numbers.

Dancing with Liam makes me feel great, but I'm still not used to drinking so fast. The lack of control doesn't sit well with me. I spend the rest of the night clearing my head of the cosmo and waiting for my friends to get tired. The girls drop me off, and I'm actually thankful that the night ended.

***

It's another chilly day in Seattle. I'm glad that Drake drives me every morning. And that we can have a little time together before school.

Actually, school has been great. I like hanging out with people my age. Being tutored wasn't horrible, but I missed the human contact. Even if my only contact is with the other castaways at Fremont High.

While Drake goes back to the car to get a paper he forgot, I walk across the parking lot. Yara's and Greta's signatures tell me they're to my left. The continuous tingling doesn't bother me. At least, unlike Jane's energy trail at our last school, it's not a constant reminder that a Night Sister may try to kill me.

Yara's skill with potions has given me an idea. I need to talk to her.

The two Sisters are chatting with Priscilla, who has her lips pursed.

"Hi, girls."

"Hey, you wild thing. We're just telling Pri about our night out," Greta says.

"It sounds like you had fun." Priscilla doesn't seem amused.

"I guess we did. Hey, Yara, a word?"

She looks at me, surprised, but she doesn't move.

"Come here." I gesture to her to follow me. We walk to an isolated patch of grass beside the building.

"What is it?" she asks.

"It's just a favor. Greta told me—and you showed me—how you're a potions prodigy. I was wondering if you could brew a few things for me. I'd pay for the ingredients, of course."

She stares at me. "Okay. What do you need? I'm guessing it's not a strong Fancy Me one, since you already have the hot boyfriend and all."

I giggle. "No, nothing like that. I haven't thought it through yet. I'll write it down, and then we can discuss it."

"Come over to my house after school. I'll show you what I can do."

"Sure, that'd be cool."

Drake comes over. "Hey, Yara." Then he kisses me. "I'm missing a page. From my paper. I'll go in and rewrite it before the bell."

"Drake, is it cool if I go to Yara's after school?"

"Oh. Weren't we…you know?" he asks.

Embarrassed, I look at Yara, but she just stares at Drake. The way she looks at him makes me uncomfortable.

She says, "Actually, I live nearby. We can walk."

I turn to him. "Can I take a rain check?"

He looks bummed, but says, "Okay." He leaves without a goodbye peck.

And I notice Yara watching him go.

***

Yara's house is a ten-minute walk from school. Greta comes with us.

We're in a brightly painted split level. Each room has a different color. The walls of the living room are turquoise; the kitchen is sunshine yellow. Yara makes us smoothies, and we chat a bit. Then we go downstairs to a vast magenta room. I try to ignore the incessant energy emanating from Yara and Greta.

"This was once my toy room," Yara says. "In a way, it still is."

"Wow! It looks like a chemistry laboratory."

"It is that also," Yara says proudly.

"Yeah, only it's pink. It's Hello Kitty's lab," Greta says.

Yara punches her on the arm. "Not cool."

Greta puts her hands up. "Hey. I like it! I had pink hair for three months."

I recognize a mortar, pestles, cauldrons, and other items every Sister has. But I also see advanced stuff: Bunsen burners, pipettes, all kinds of containers, test tubes, and flasks.

"What are those?" I ask, looking at some pieces of equipment in a corner.

"Kettles, kiln, filters, evaporators." Yara points at each item in turn.

"It's more loaded than the science lab at school! Your parents know you're a Sister, right?" It'd be hard to explain why a teenage girl would need a state-of-the-art pharmaceutical lab.

"They know. Mom is one too. And Dad is the one who made a fuss about buying all kinds of insurance for the house." Yara bites her lip. "Accidents do happen."

"Show her the *real* lab," Greta says.

Yara leads us to the adjacent room. It has a door with a window. "This is a sterile room. For finer mixtures."

It's the only dull-painted room in the house. Save for a few silvery machines and some transparent vials, everything is white. I look at Yara with genuine admiration. She is so quiet at school, but her eyes light up while she shows me the room.

"And there?" I point to the next door.

"That's just the laundry room. And the bathroom, and the garage. Not important."

She explains why the room is perfect for her. She spray-painted the small windows in the front, so no one can peek inside. The outside light comes from the sliding doors that lead to the backyard. "Very useful, because I had to run outside with some potions that didn't work out. The grass is dead around the porch from all the...unsuccessful trials."

"She uses the fireplace too," Greta says.

Yara shrugs. "It's good to air the fumes. And here's my pantry." She taps a large apothecary cabinet. It has a multitude of small drawers, all of them labeled. Then she sits at a small computer desk and opens her laptop. "So I can do almost anything. What do you need?"

Chapter 14: Drake

Our little gang is seated in an unlit, isolated, and forgotten corner of the cafeteria. A very metaphorical table.

Boulder's rage continues to simmer. "This is not working," he says, gesturing broadly. He has a cheeseburger in one hand and a box of Muscle Milk in the other.

Priscilla says, "I don't see what the big problem is. I went from having no friends at Greenwood High to having no friends at Fremont High. Same difference."

I try to lighten up the mood. "Come on, Priscilla, our non-friends there were much better than our non-friends here."

"It's not about friends," Boulder says, pointing his sandwich at me. "It's about respect."

Priscilla sighs. "Again, I went from having no respect—"

"Not true!" Boulder is adamant. "We had respect, Pri. People might not talk to you, but everybody envied your body."

Sean snickers. "Smooth, big guy."

"It's the truth. And they envied my physique too—"

I interrupt him. "Your 'physique'?"

Sean loses it.

Boulder ignores both of us. "...as well as my personality—"

It's Priscilla's turn to interrupt him. "Your 'personality'?"

This time he stops and stares at her. "Don't diss my personality, sweetheart. Not too long ago, you were smitten with it."

"Or maybe I was smitten with your *physique*?"

Sean's uproarious laugh attracts a lot of attention to our table. But Fremont High is not used to his antics yet. A couple of guys glare at us; a girl rolls her eyes. Somehow, we drop further on the popularity scale.

Boulder punches Sean on the shoulder, splashing Muscle Milk on me. "You are not helping, Sean," Boulder hisses. "We need a plan. Some way of getting them on our side."

Greta and Yara, the witches, enter the cafeteria. Greta waves at us.

Skye, who has been silent during Boulder's rant, waves back and motions them to join us.

Greta says something to Yara, who shrugs. The two of them approach our table.

"They don't mind us," I say. "That's a start."

"Oh, please," Sean snickers. "The Weird Sisters? How are they helping our cause?"

"I didn't realize we were a cause," I reply, offended for me and for the witches.

Sean just shakes his head.

Greta arrives and says, "Hey, guys. Got into any fights since the bell?"

Yara just gives a nod aimed at all of us and buries her nose in her cell again.

"Not yet," Skye replies. "Come on, sit down. I mean, if it's okay?" Skye looks around the cafeteria.

Greta says, "Well, it *is* the losers table, but the usual losers are avoiding it today."

"Great," Boulder mumbles. "We've reached rock bottom. Lower than dorks."

"I can't imagine why," Greta replies. "But I don't care about status." She sits down.

When did sitting down at a cafeteria table turn into a stand, a gesture of bravery? When Greta does it, there's a certain dignity to it, even. I become a Greta fan instantly.

Greta pulls down on Yara's arm, who sits down without taking her eyes off of the screen. Greta turns to Boulder. "I've inquired about you. Kids here know you. From football and parties."

Boulder suddenly becomes interested in what the Weird Sister has to say. "Really?"

"I've heard a lot of stories about you," she says, suppressing a smile.

He grins.

The rest of us are only spectators now. Greta and Boulder are center stage.

"So you have the fame. What you need," she continues, "is to earn their respect."

His eyes bulge. He faces each of us in turn. "What did I tell you guys? She gets it!"

She goes on. "So this talk of parties had me thinking. Why don't you throw a party for Fremont High?"

Boulder opens his mouth slightly. "That's...awesome! That's perfect, actually."

Greta tilts her head to the side and smiles softly as if to say, "I know."

He drops his sandwich, leans over the table, and clasps her hand with his massive paw. "What did you say your name was, again?"

"I didn't. It's Greta."

"Greta. Would you like to come to a party at my house?"

"Just tell me when, big guy."

***

It's almost dusk. Skye is leaving my house. "Are you sure?" I ask. "I can drive you home."

She shakes her head. "No, I have to stop by the park now." She lowers her eyes. "Perform a quick ritual, you know."

"Oh, now I'm more comfortable. Sneaking into the park alone after dark? Did you forget the witch following you the other day?"

Skye smirks. "I can defend myself."

"I know." I kiss her.

She pushes me away gently and giggles. "I've got to go." Then she opens the door and walks down the street while I watch her.

My life has become awfully strange.

I stay there for a few minutes, ignoring the chilly breeze. My eyes catch a girl walking toward my house. My little sister Mona. After she gained magical powers, she became gorgeous. She tries to hide her newfound beauty with the black outfits, but it's still noticeable.

"You just missed Skye," I tell Mona when she climbs the front steps. "She was worried about you."

She passes by me and enters the living room. "I'm constantly worried about her well-being too. I mean, she dates *you*."

"Seriously, Mona. You know that Jane is out there, and she knows you're the Singularity. And you walk home alone after dark. Couldn't Pain's parents give you a ride? You can call me too, you know? I'd pick you up at Pain's."

She blinks a little too fast. "Aren't you too freaked out?"

70

"I just don't want to see you getting hurt. Or worse."

I wish it was a joke. Jane tried to kill both Skye and Mona last month. Jane and the Night covens want to steal Mona's uncanny powers. It's just a matter of time before the Night witches come knocking and try to kidnap my sister.

But Mona and Skye think it's okay to wander Seattle's streets alone.

Mona drops her black purse on the sofa and leans on the wall. "You're right, Drake."

Of all the weird things happening, my sister saying I'm right must be one of the strangest. "Are you serious?" I ask.

She walks away from the wall and sits on the sofa. "I've been thinking. Skye gave me Shield and Protection potions, but I don't know if they're going to hold up when the Night covens come for me." Her voice is surprisingly even.

"*If* they come for you."

Mona squints at me. "No. It's *when*, Drake. Pain and I have been discussing it for a while. By now, Jane must have told the Night covens that I'm the real Singularity. They must be planning it carefully, in case I create another accidental earthquake again. Or another fire. They want to be ready. Then I'll be taken, dead or alive."

Her matter-of-fact demeanor is startling. This is not the Mona I know.

"I'm sorry that you have to go through this, Mona."

"It's not your fault." Her lips smile, but her eyes don't. "I need to learn more from Skye. I need to use my own magic, so I know how to defend myself."

"If you use your magic, they'll sense it immediately."

"There must be a way of doing magic and shielding the magical signature. If I'm as powerful as they say, I should be able to figure it out, right? I need to fight them on my own. I don't want to put you all on the line again."

"I'll help you. I'm your big brother."

She nods. "I know. For the record, you're an okay big brother."

Chapter 15: Skye

Greta and I are at Yara's house again. This time, Yara has closed the curtains on the sliding door. She shows me an orange plastic bag.

"Here's your order. Goddess, I feel like a drug dealer."

"Don't say that," Greta admonishes her.

Yara looks at her and opens her mouth, but says nothing. She turns to me and removes a blue pillbox from the bag. "You asked for a lot of potions. It'd be a big volume, so I just pressed them into pills. Easy to carry, easy to store, easy to conceal." She gives me a meaningful look.

"That's...genius." I hold up a pill against the light. It looks like a multi-vitamin pill: gray with faint green dots. "I've heard of potion pills, but I've never seen them."

"I color-coded them so you'll know how to differentiate: green are Shield; red are Protection; purple are Stamina; orange are Healing."

"What about the others?"

"Since I imagined you would be the one taking the protective ones, I made them into pills. But the attack potions have to be delivered in another form. Unless you can force your target to swallow a pill."

Nodding, I say, "I've used Sleep, Decay, and Blinding as throwing potions."

Greta's eyes widen. "When?"

I hesitate, but end up sharing. "I had to fight Jane once."

Yara is surprised, but she continues, "Yes, since they are topical, I guess you can throw them. I mean, if you want to behave like a barbarian. My delivery methods are more sophisticated."

Greta laughs.

Yara ignores her. "You didn't ask for it, but I prepared a sampler. A lipstick collection with Sleep, Fancy Me, Forget, and Truth. For the vixen in all of us."

I smile.

Yara is loving this. "If you can't kiss the target, you need an alternative. It's a shame you don't smoke: I could have prepared cigarettes. I thought about nail polish, but I noticed you don't use it often. So I created this." She takes a spray bottle out of the bag. "Same potions in aerosol form."

"This…this is incredible, Yara."

"She has a Potions Charm. And she takes advanced chem classes," Greta says.

Yara beams. "Wait, but that's not all. You also get my little masterpiece."

"Is that a temporary tattoo?"

"Yes!" she squeals. "Sorry. This is the coolest thing ever. The tattoo ink is laced with a potion. When you apply the tattoo, the potion is protected with a microfilm. If you want to use the potion, just disrupt the microfilm—any scratch will do—and the potion will be in touch with your skin. The best way of sneaking a potion anywhere."

"You could be stripped naked and still carry a potion with you,"

Greta says.

"Thank you, Q!"

The two of them stare at me blankly.

"Q? The gadget guy from James Bond? Never mind. I'm impressed! What's the potion laced in the tattoo?"

"Dispel," Yara says quietly.

"You know Dispel?" I'm stunned. This is one of the most powerful potions or spells a Sister can learn. It basically negates the effects of another potion or spell. I don't even know the ingredients, but I've heard they are crazy expensive.

"I went to Salvador last summer just to learn it."

Greta puts her hands around her friend's shoulders. "That's in Brazil. Yara's grandma is the Eldest Mother there. She taught our little genius."

Yara's cheeks become pink. "I'm not a genius at all. I wish I had an Intellect Charm. I have Potions and Allure. I'm actually grounded because my grades are so bad."

"That, and your piercing," Greta adds.

"Thank you, Greta, for sharing my few secrets with the world." She turns to me again. "This Dispel is infused with my own personal magic, so it's not too powerful. But it should be enough for a regular spell. And you must remember: a Dispel cannot counter a Charm. Dispel only works on potions and other spells."

"Thank you so much! I'll pay for the ingredients and everything. And I'll owe you one."

She nods, but gives me a look. "You still didn't tell me why you need this arsenal."

The two Sisters become serious.

"They're for a friend," I tell them.

***

Again, Mona can't relax. Who would blame her?

She's in front of me, trying to focus. Her goth makeup—white base, black eyeliner, and purple lipstick—goes well with her dark clothes. And when she closes her eyes to meditate, I can see the violet eye shadow. She could be the poster girl for *Seventeen Witch*, if the magazine existed.

We're alone in my room. Aunt Gemma is out for the day. This is a great chance to teach Mona some basic rituals.

"It's okay, Mona. We don't have to do much today. Have you been doing the relaxation exercises?"

"Yes, but this is different."

"We'll try to take you to a meditative state, and then let some of your magical energy flow. Just a bit," I say, showing her my thumb and index finger almost touching.

"I just don't know how I can feel the magic, and at the same time, not let it out of my body."

I pat her shoulder. "You'll be fine. You did it when we healed Drake and Brianna after the fire. Just remember how you did it."

"Skye, this is different. That time you told me it was okay to let the energy flow a little, because the Sisters thought it was coming from Brianna. But now you're asking me to not let *anything* out."

"You're just afraid to try, but I know you can do it. That night, you were in complete shock. Let me see: you had unintentionally created an earthquake and a fire; you had been kidnapped and almost died. And yet you *still* controlled your magical energy and fed me just the right amount for our commune ritual. This will be easy for you."

Mona stares at me and nods. She squeezes her eyes shut at first, but soon relaxes her facial muscles. Her breathing becomes steady.

It's just the beginning. She needs to be trained to use just the amount of magic a regular Sister would.

I give her a few minutes while I put away the herbs I was showing her. Then I wait.

"I can sense it," she whispers. "I think I can do it."

Even with True Sight and so close to her, I don't sense her signature. She's doing well.

"Okay," I say softly. "Now, let out just a tiny bit."

"How? Should we hold hands?"

"No, that was for our commune ritual. Now you must do it by yourself. Focus on a small part of your body. Let it flow slowly from your fingertips."

I feel it. It's not overwhelming, but definitely too much. "Easy," I say. "A little less."

Instead, the flow increases. Not much, but definitely over a regular Sister's signature. It reaches me in a sudden burst, and I groan. With my True Sight and the proximity, it hits me hard.

The surge worries me. "Just breathe, Mona." My calm voice masks my concern. If she loses control completely, we're done.

The energy decreases slowly. With her so close to me, the energy is still high, but about what an average Sister would release naturally.

"That's it. Hold it for a minute."

She does as told. Her control is improving.

"You're doing great. Now try to rein it in."

The tingling diminishes rapidly, and then it's gone.

Mona opens her eyes. "That was incredible!"

"It was. But you still need to control it better."

Mona's smile wavers. "I tried to."

"Sorry. You did exactly what you're supposed to do. Remember that energy level at the end; that's how much you should use in your rituals. But you can only do magic if you're alone: nobody can know you're a Sister."

"And when do I learn those rituals?"

"Easy, grasshopper. For today, let's just practice holding the energy level."

Mona purses her lips, but nods.

Chapter 16: Drake

I wake up in the middle of the night. In the dark house, I hear the faint but distinct sound of people talking. I decide to go downstairs to check it out.

The TV is on, Sportscenter playing in a loop through the night. On the sofa, Dad is sleeping, an almost imperceptible snoring joining the droning of the TV. His breathing is intermittent.

"I promise," he mumbles.

"What?" I ask.

But he's not awake. He's dreaming. "I'll keep an eye on them."

Despite the guilt eavesdropping on his dream brings, I cannot stop listening.

"Please," Dad mutters. "Stay."

He's dreaming of...Mom. The sorrow I felt a few minutes earlier comes back. I feel bad about invading his privacy. I slink to the kitchen, get a tall glass of water, and go back to bed.

Sleep never comes.

***

The swim team practice is over. I cool down in the pool while my teammates go to the locker rooms to hit the showers. They chat among themselves, but I'm the new guy. Coach Summers gives me a thumbs-up and leaves for the day.

I leave the pool and practice my starts. Since I never swam in competitions, I never bothered to learn the proper technique on how to enter the water. An imaginary bell sounds in my head, and I dive. Then I go back up and do it over and over again. I've got so many new things to learn: posture, how to bend your knees, proper foot position, correct impulse, the right angle of entering the water.

The other swimmers have finished their showers. They are leaving the pool building. These guys have known how to dive since they were little. I have to catch up.

It's not the pressure I thought it would be. The repetition of diving, analyzing the movement, and trying again is actually soothing.

I decide to do a few more laps at my own pace, just like I used to before joining the team. It relaxes me. I don't care about turns—something else I need to practice—during *my* laps. I tap one end and swim back.

After one of those laps, I see someone in the stands. A girl. Yara.

I go back and forth one more time, but I can't stop wondering what she's doing here. I reach for the ladder and come out of the pool.

She leaves her seat and approaches me.

"Hey, D," she says, all smiles. Her eyes scan me from head to toe.

"Hey, Yara." I wrap a towel around my waist. "So, visiting Greenwood?"

"Yep," she replies, still staring at my chest. "It's the place where the famous Singularity was found, isn't it? Soon this will be a pilgrimage place for the Sisters."

I want to remind her that my eyes are up here, but I don't want to be rude. Or presumptuous. "That's a bit of an overstatement."

"She dated you, didn't she? The Singularity," she says, getting close to me. I instinctively bring my towel up, like a heroine of the old classics trying to hide her modesty.

Having her body so near to mine is unnerving. She is a beautiful girl—I can't deny it. Underneath her open jacket, she wears a tight pink tank top that is crying for attention.

I keep my voice flat. "We kissed once. How do you know?"

"I have chem with a couple of your Greenwood classmates. They told me you had a reputation. 'KK'."

"'KK'?"

"The Kissing King. That's what they told me." She makes a naughty face.

I laugh. "This is ridiculous," I say. "They couldn't know."

"Why?"

"Let's just say the sampling size is too small to have a reputation."

"Want to increase the sample size then?"

She gets close. As in crazy close, a few molecules apart, and she puts a hand on my chest. Her hand is warm against my cold, wet skin. I take a step back, but realize I'm close to the wall. I'm trapped.

"Look, Yara. I have a girlfriend."

"It's just a kiss. Would you deny a girl a taste?"

"Come on. This is not cool," I say. My voice is serious now.

Yara removes her hand and retreats, making way for me. "It's just a kiss, D. You don't need to be so uptight. It's not a big deal."

"It kind of is. To me."

Her disappointed eyes stare at me. "Okay, I get it." She turns and walks away. "I'm leaving."

I don't want this to become a problem. Maybe she got the message. Slowly, I make my way to the locker room.

Before she leaves the building, she yells from the lobby. "Maybe you'd be better off locking the door to the showers. Just to be safe."

I collect my things from my locker and drive away. I'll shower at home.

Chapter 17: Skye

"We're getting ahead of ourselves," I tell Mona. "Magic is just a small part of the Craft; the real essence of what makes a Sister a witch is the philosophy of the covens."

Mona winces. "Philosophy? Really?"

"I mean the ideas behind it. It won't be a boring college course, I promise."

Ravenna Park is a perfect place to discuss it. Once more, Seattle's abundance of verdant spaces help me attune to the Craft.

"Like in many other religions, the Sisters believe that all living things are interconnected. We all have this energy within us. We must respect life, but of course we must take into account that things change—the modern world and the evolution of the human race. I'm a vegetarian, for example, but not all Sisters are."

Mona nods.

I go on. "Some of us, like me, believe in a deity, the Goddess. But others think it's just a…symbol, an icon, not a real goddess. Like Mother Nature. Others are sure that the Goddess is a manifestation of magical energy. There's no right or wrong explanation. You need to discover what's true to *you*. This is something that you'll figure out for yourself."

"It sounds like Wicca."

"Wicca is pretty close to the real Craft. Wiccans, like Sisters, disagree in some aspects of the tenets, like the true nature of the Goddess. But they all agree that we all have this energy inside of us. The main difference is that true witches can use this energy much more effectively."

A girl approaches us. She is jogging and wearing a short skirt and long-sleeved shirt. The earphones put me at ease. She can't overhear us.

"We can tap into this internal energy," I say. "This is magic. When a Sister reaches Daybreak, an outburst of energy tells her she's ready to practice magic. The Charms then 'turn on'—and we can start infusing spells and potions with our personal magic."

"How are Charms different from spells and potions?"

"Charms are always on and never release magical energy. Our Allure doesn't go away when we're sleeping. All your Charms stay on."

"I lit a match and tested the Fire Immunity the other day," Mona says with a sly expression. "Don't tell Drake."

"I knew you'd try it. I would too. Don't worry; Charms don't trigger any witch alarms."

"What else?"

"I don't know everything. Sorry, Mona, but you drew the short straw. Those things are usually taught by the Mothers. They have studied their whole lives. I'm only a little ahead of you on the Craft. I know what most Sisters my age would—and a little more, because Judi and Mum are good teachers. I can teach you the tenets, the basics, and just a few advanced things. I could train a Sister who wasn't raised as one, but you... Everything I know, I'll share with you, okay?"

Mona doesn't sound disappointed. "Awesome. I need all the help I can get."

"We need to figure out your Charms," I tell Mona. "We all have two. I have Allure and True Sight. Mum has Allure and Charisma."

"Is Allure the most common?" she asks.

"Yes. We already know you have it."

"Jane didn't have it. She had Steal," Mona says.

"I don't even know what it is called. Very rare. But 'Steal' sounds about right." The mention of Jane throws me a little, but then I remember Mona doesn't know many Sisters.

"How could she steal my magic?"

I hesitate, but she needs to hear it. "When a Sister dies, her magic returns to the Goddess. Some say it returns to the Cosmos, Earth, or Nature. The point is, the magical energy goes back to the universal pool. Jane's Charm can capture magical energy before that. It can also temporarily hijack one's Charm."

"Like your True Sight?"

"Right. My Charm lets me see auras if I use this." I tap my glasses with rainbow-colored lenses.

"Can I see them?"

I hand them over. She weighs them on her hand and then looks at them against the bedroom light. Then she puts them on.

"Whoa!"

"What?" I ask.

"You have a glow around your head."

"For real? Mona, you may have True Sight too. If you do, you'd have three: Fire Immunity, Allure, and this one. Can you sense me?"

"No."

"No? Like a tingling sensation all over your body?"

"Nothing."

I expected to be disappointed, but the reality is I'm a little relieved. True Sight has always been *my* thing. It almost defines me. That's why they selected me for the Search, after all.

Wow, I didn't know I could be that selfish. Still, Mona has power in spades; it's not like she won't have magic to spare.

"Can I take them to school? They're not prescription."

Of course, she's excited. The energy and magical effects are almost always unidentifiable, invisible. Especially for her, when she cannot use the Craft at all, it must be something to see auras around people.

"Sure, but take care of them. This is my new pair, custom-made for me."

She turns her head around, looking at trees and bushes.

"It only works on people and animals," I volunteer.

"Oh." She takes them off and puts them inside the case I hand to her. "Now what?"

"I'm still trying to figure out how your powers work. Charms are supposed to be always on, like your Allure. So if you had True Sight, it'd be on right now, and my signature so close to you would overwhelm you. So it's Aura Sight Charm."

"Only Aura Sight?"

"'Only?' It's great. Useful too. The important thing is: this is your third Charm! I never knew someone could have three. You…"

"What about me?"

"The things you can do are unheard of. You may have other Charms manifesting right now, and I couldn't identify them. I might not even notice them. You are such an outlier, I cannot understand some things that are going on."

She giggles. "You know how to boost an ego, don't you?"

I smile. "I mean it. In the past—like, hundreds and thousands of years ago, the Sisters were more powerful. I wish I knew more about the Sisters' history, so I could understand your powers."

"Maybe you could ask your mother. Or Judi."

Smart girl. "Good point. But I need to figure out how to raise the subject without making them suspicious."

I'm proud of Mona in a strange way. Training her makes me see myself as a teacher. I'm growing up. Taking on responsibility. Which is true: since I've made the decision to not hand her over to the covens, I'm responsible for her.

"Here, I have something for you." I take a necklace with a pendant from my pocket.

"A pentagram? That's totally me! Thanks, Skye."

"It's not jewelry. Well, it was. Before I infused it with a spell. Now it's an amulet."

Her eyes go big. "A magical amulet? Are you kidding me?" She snatches the necklace from my hands. "What does it do?"

I love her enthusiasm. "It is a Protection amulet. It's as if a Protection spell is always on. It helps with deflecting malignant spells and potions. It's not that powerful; it only has my personal magic, so don't rely on it. It can slow down, but not contain Night magic spells completely. Night magic would probably be stronger than my pitiful necklace."

Mona holds it against the sky, examining every detail of the pendant. It's a simple pewter pentagram inscribed in a circle.

She tries to put it on but can't quite navigate the clasp. She turns, and I do it for her. "Is Night magic stronger in general?"

"Yes. They are not afraid to dig deeper into the primal aspects of energy."

"What do you mean?"

"A Night Sister may kill animals during her rituals, for example, and use their energy in tandem with hers and their blood in potions. Some of us believe spirits, or beings of magical energy, are around us. Night Sisters call on them, invoking their energy. This makes for powerful magic, but it's tainted magic. That's not what the Craft is about. The true Craft celebrates life. Always remember that."

***

I'm distracted by the drizzling rain hitting the windshield. The metronomic sound the wipers make is trying to put me to sleep.

Drake and I remain silent. It's good not having to talk. We're both comfortable with it, at least for a while. Later, I plan to cozy up to Drake, though. I'm not made of steel.

He's driving me to a Wiccan shop. I can get my supplies—herbs, mostly—from them.

A small electric current starts to spread along my spine. "A Sister is approaching," I say, turning to look through the back window. It's foggy, though.

"Your spider sense?"

"Yep."

He looks at the rearview and side mirrors. "Doesn't that happen often, though? I mean, your reach is wider; you probably pick up witch energy all the time."

"There aren't that many witches. Sometimes I sense one, but they're usually far away and their energy fades as we move. Now we're in a moving car, and the energy is constant." I look back to the road.

"Do you think someone is following us?" he asks.

"Maybe."

"Jane?"

"Maybe. I can't see a motorcycle, but it doesn't mean anything. She lost hers, remember? And she could be driving. Slow down." I put my hand on his arm.

"Anything?"

"The energy is level. But I cannot see which car it is."

"Let me try something."

He swerves to changes lanes and turns left when the opposing traffic slows down.

The energy barely fluctuates. "She's still behind us. About the same intensity. She's keeping a distance, which means she knows I'm a Sister, but doesn't know about my True Sight."

Drake tries a few more unexpected turns, but our pursuer keeps following us.

"Can you see the car?" I ask.

"No. We could go to streets with less traffic. Or stop altogether. Why would someone follow you? If it's Jane, she knows where to find us."

I'm trying to come up with a plan. "Let's bait her. Drop me off somewhere. If she's following me, you can go around her and figure out who she is."

"Maybe she is following me," he says.

"Then why would she stay just out of a regular Sister's range?"

"Good point. Okay, but I won't leave you at just any place. You need to be safe. Can't be your house, because she may be looking for where you live. Pri's house?"

"No, she's texted me; she's at the mall. Yara's house?"

"Won't you confuse her signature with the bad guy's?"

"No, I can sense direction and intensity. But Yara would be suspicious. We need a public place, but not a crowd. We need to figure out who she is."

He makes a sharp turn. "I know. I'll drop you off around the corner and keep going. She'll follow me, but maybe you can get a look at her."

"She'll sense me when she's close."

"I have no other ideas. Let's trap her," he says.

Drake speeds and makes another turn near a gas station. He brakes, and I get out of the car even before he comes to a total stop. I slam the door shut, and off he goes.

Hiding behind the wall of a shop, still in the rain, I wait for our pursuer. I ready my cell phone and point the camera to the road. She's close enough that she can sense me. Then I spot her. The same silver Ford Focus I saw at Mona's dance. It approaches the corner. The woman driving is looking around, probably searching for me, the source of energy.

Something comes over me, and I step forward, in plain view of her. We lock eyes, and I snap a picture.

She swerves left all of a sudden—in the opposite direction Drake went. A car brakes, avoiding a collision, and honks at her, but she's gone. I punch in the plate numbers on my cell, just in case the picture didn't get it. Then I call Drake.

"She's gone."

"I'm picking you up," he says.

While I wait, I zoom in on the shot. Her face is blurred, the rain-drenched windshield hiding her features. The phone's camera is not good, and she was going fast, trying to catch up to Drake.

Drake parks in front of me, and I get in.

"I got a picture of her, but I cannot see her face. I have her plates, though."

"Good. Let me take a look. Ugh, it's all fuzzy."

"Well, it's clear it's not Jane. It's just one Sister." I dry the rain water from my face with my sleeves.

He looks at me. "A Night Sister."

"Yep. And I bet she's wondering how we detected she was following us. She knows—her coven knows—that we saw them. Maybe this will force them to make a move."

"We need to be ready," Drake says with gritted teeth. He takes to the road again, his hands on the wheel in a tight grip.

Chapter 18: Drake

A terrible dream ambushed me tonight. Brianna had woken up and outed Mona as the Singularity. Witches dressed in black and white were pulling Mona by the arms and legs, until she tore apart in a bloody mess. I was there, paralyzed and full of despair.

I wake up with a shudder, gasping for air. The image stays with me for a while.

A quiet sadness overtakes me. I cannot forget what I have just dreamed. I take a long shower before going downstairs for breakfast.

In search of a less stressful time, I call Boulder and invite myself over. When I arrive there, Sean is already spread on the futon, eating a snack, eyes on the ceiling, while Boulder hammers on the laptop.

"Hey, Boulder."

"Shh," he says, raising a finger, not even looking at me.

The snub doesn't offend me. I turn my attention to Sean. "Hey, Sean. How are the screenwriting classes?"

"Doing well," he answers with his mouth full. "Right now, I'm working on an action movie. Die Hard in Disneyland."

I grin. "Sounds awesome."

"I know, right? I also have this idea of a sequel to Jurassic Park, only the raptors now know how to hold and shoot guns."

"I'd definitely pay to see that."

"What about you? What have you been doing?"

"Besides the missus," Boulder mumbles from the desk.

I ignore the bait. "Nothing much. Swimming again. What are you eating?" I ask Sean.

"Gummy bears."

"Those aren't gummy bears. Those are gummy vites."

"What's the difference?"

"They're toddler's vitamins!"

"So?"

"So you're eating almost a full bottle. It'll make you sick."

"Dude, it's vitamins. It can only be good for you. And I weigh like two hundred times a toddler."

"You'll get sick. And you need to improve your math skills."

"I just like them."

"Why can't you eat undetermined ground meat like the rest of us?"

"I like gummy bears."

He does, and he keeps eating them as if time has stopped and nothing else matters.

"Don't you worry about anything?" I ask.

"Of course not. Do you?"

I have nothing to say. Boulder is looking at Sean as if he's crazy.

"What, big guy?' Sean asks. "Your life's perfect. What do *you* have to worry about?"

Boulder shakes his head and goes back to the computer.

Chapter 19: Skye

The stroll in the park left us both freezing. Drake suggests a coffee, and we walk toward one of Fremont's local coffeehouses.

"Who do you imagine your mother is?" I ask.

"I never do."

"Of course you do."

"Okay, I used to. Not anymore. But, for a while, I imagined—no, I wished—that she was a spy. That she had to give us up for the sake of the country or to ensure world peace. And that she lived this mysterious life, full of peril, with the memory of us as the only thing keeping her from breaking apart. And, of course, that she's been keeping tabs on us the whole time."

"Loving you from afar but keeping watch?"

He says nothing.

"You're a romantic."

"Silly, huh?"

"No, you have an active—and ambitious—imagination."

Drake snorts. "Can you blame me? My girlfriend is an honest-to goodness witch. If that is possible, other wonderful things can happen too."

We arrive at the coffeehouse, and Drake opens the door for me.

While we wait in line, I look around the quaint café. Small, unframed paintings cover the walls. They're all for sale. One artist overuses the color red in abstract images. Another one paints Cubist vistas of Seattle: who knew a geometric troll could look cute?

Drake is looking through the unwashed window. He says to me, "Be right back," and goes outside.

The line moves. I'm curious and follow him with my eyes. He approaches a scruffy guy sitting on the sidewalk. The man wears a worn-out winter jacket and ripped jeans.

Drake crouches and talks to the man, who's startled at first but soon answers. Drake reaches into his pocket and hands him a few dollar bills.

The line moves again, and I order at last.

Outside, my boyfriend is returning. The man glances at the bills, but looks back at Drake and stares at him walking back into the café.

I quickly find a table and sit before Drake sees me watching him.

Drake enters, finds me, and sits down.

"I didn't know what you wanted," I say.

"It's okay."

"Aren't you going to order something? You said you were dying for a coffee."

"Changed my mind." He shrugs.

Did he give away all his cash? "I can get you one." I move to stand up.

He holds my arm gently. "No, it's fine," he says, smiling.

I smile back, but this reminds me again of the difference in our families' wealth. He won't accept me paying for anything. Going dutch, yes, but not treating him.

"Wanna share?" I hand him the hot cup.

He hesitates, but takes a tiny sip and gives the cup back to me.

When we leave the coffeehouse, the man's still there. He just gives a brief nod at Drake. He says nothing about it. Neither do I.

***

Mona is progressing with her Craft lessons. I'm happy for her—and a little proud of myself. I may be a good teacher.

Still, I'm troubled by her lack of progress in controlling her energy. This is key. If I cannot teach her to do it consistently, there's no point in teaching her rituals: she would release another outburst of magical energy and attract all the Sisters in the Pacific Northwest.

This morning she is upbeat. She's wearing my special glasses.

"How do you like those?" I ask.

"Oh, they're incredible. I've been staring at everyone. I'm a creep."

"Found out anything?"

She nods. "I've used what you told me: the inner aura is the nature, the outer one is the how they're feeling. I've even made a table with the colors."

"So you're one of those students who writes everything down?" I chuckle.

"Only for this. Look: Dad has a green one, with a blue outer. Most girls at school have an orange, and a few are pink."

"Pink is always good—what Judi used to call a 'healthy soul,' but your father looks worried about something."

"What else is new? Here's Drake's: pink with a deep red. What does it mean?"

I gasp. I could never see Drake's aura for some reason, but it never occurred to me to ask Mona to "spy" for me.

"Skye?"

"It's love," I mumble. "Deep love."

Mona's reaction is unexpected. I thought she would tease me, or congratulate me, or maybe squeal. But she just looks more stunned than I am.

"Is that okay?"

She stares at me. "Yeah, yeah. I'm glad for you," she says in a rush of words.

"Mona, are you sure? What else is going on?"

"It's nothing."

"You can tell me."

She hesitates. "It's just...Pain tells me everything. But her aura is even redder than Drake's. And she never told me anything about anyone."

I understand what she is saying, but I refrain from talking about it. We stay in silence for a while, both pondering what those deep red auras mean—and how we are going to handle the people close to us.

***

When I get back home, I'm greeted by the unlikeliest of visitors: Connor.

"How are you doing, Skye?"

He's sitting on the sofa across from Aunt Gemma. They're having tea and chatting like old pals. A tray of biscuits is on the coffee table.

"Connor had the courtesy of paying me a visit," Gemma says. "I had forgotten how charming he is."

He displays his toothpaste-ad smile. "My pleasure. But I must apologize. I have been so busy that I didn't have time to sit down with one of my favorite Knowings."

Aunt Gemma lets out a satisfied giggle. Don't be entranced by him, Aunt. I was once, and I got hurt.

"I'm happy to have you here," she says. "Finally, a distinguished visitor."

This is a disguised dig at my only other visitors: Priscilla, deemed by Aunt Gemma as "that loose girl," and Drake, not referred to at all.

"Connor, this is a surprise," I say at last.

"Since you are here, I'd like to talk to you. Gemma, this is coven business, would you mind giving us the room?" His command is delivered with a smile.

"Of course. I'll be upstairs." She shoots him a glance as if they are saying goodbye on the deck of the Titanic.

"So, making the rounds, huh?" I tease Connor when she's gone.

"It's good politics, Skye. And she is a delight."

"Just because she worships you." I raise my eyebrows.

"That has something to do with it, yes." He grins. "But I'm glad I caught up with you. As it turns out, Elsa Dunivant cannot travel anymore."

I try to conceal my relief. "Really? You mean, the Mother with Truth Charm?"

"Yes. She's not that young, and we're having trouble finding someone else with Truth."

"That's too bad. I was looking forward to it." I'm shameless.

Connor leans back on the sofa. "Oh, don't be worried. You will travel there to meet her later. Meanwhile, we will take your statement here. You don't mind taking a Truth potion, do you? It's not the same thing—the Truth Charm cannot be countered, but in this case, a potion will have to do for the time being."

My blood freezes. I thought I was scot-free. But he's right. I can beat a potion with one of Yara's Dispels. Not a Charm, though. Charms are immune to Dispels.

He adds, "I'll let you know when."

I snap out of my brain stoppage. "Yeah. Sure. But my calendar is pretty busy."

He narrows his eyes, but still smiles. "Is it?"

"Yes. New school and all. Parties. New friends. Boyfriend."

"Still dating?"

"Connor, we talked about it. I can't—"

He raises his palms. "No, no. Sorry. I didn't mean it that way. I just want you to know I am willing to give us another shot. If you are."

His eyes pierce me with sincerity; it's not just his Trust Charm at work.

"Connor—"

"Just leave the possibility open. That's all I ask," he whispers.

It's weird rebuffing him again. I should end it, but it's cruel destroying his hopes just like that. I nod.

His face relaxes, and Connor tells me he needs to leave. This time, when he kisses me goodbye on the cheek, I blush the slightest of pinks.

What's wrong with me?

Chapter 20: Drake

We're all checking our phones when the Kidd Valley girl calls "Boul—Bal—Boulder?"

I look up and see her frowning at the receipt slip.

Sean says, "It's ready, big man."

"Then go get it," Boulder replies.

They still have their eyes on their phones.

"They called your name," Sean says.

"I order; you pick up."

"No. You order; you go."

"It's the order for the whole table."

"Just go."

Skye slaps the table. "Oh, for Goddess' sake! I'll go." She rises.

"Do you need help?" I ask her.

"I've got it," she says, already on her way.

Her outburst finally makes them forget their phones. "Did she just say 'Goddess'?" Sean asks.

I try to save her. "She said 'goodness.' It's her accent."

"Accent? She's got almost no accent," Sean says. "Weird."

When I glance over at the counter, I see Skye trying to balance two full trays. Seven sandwiches, tons of fries, and an army of soda cups. I'm about to get up and help her, but she sees me and shakes her head.

"Skye?" I ask, pointing to the trays.

"I've got it!" she insists.

She can manage. She doesn't need my help.

She doesn't need my help. This stays with me while my friends attack the food. Since I first met her, right after she arrived in Seattle, she seems to have the hang of many things. Her confidence shot up, and she knows what she wants. I'm glad one of the things she wants is me.

"Hey, zombie boyfriend," she says. "Your ground animal is getting cold."

Sean pauses, his open mouth about to get a bite. "Skye. Please."

She giggles. Skye has changed so much in the past few weeks.

***

The annoying honk can only mean one thing: the guys are here to pick me up. And my clean t-shirts are hiding or something. The Hendrix shirt I wore yesterday is a candidate. I sniff it and put it on. It'll have to do. It's only us guys anyway.

The honking is back. Just one long honk, like a factory's siren.

"Stop it!" Mona yells.

I look out the window. Mona is in front of the house, hands on her hips.

"Sorry," Boulder says. "Did I wake you, little girl? Didn't know it was naptime."

My sister throws her hands up in the air and stomps back into the house.

I leave the bedroom and pass her coming up the stairs. I ask her, "Why isn't the laundry done?"

"Because it was your turn to do it, dummy!"

Oh. Right.

After I grab my jacket, I climb into the back seat.

"You could just text, you know?" I say, shoving my cell in Boulder's face.

"Who has the time?" Boulder swats my arm away and starts driving.

"Right. Guess who Mona will blame for it?"

Sean turns in the seat. "Mona is looking good, D-Man! You be careful."

"Thank you, pervert. She can take care of herself."

"I'll never hit on her, Drake. Damn! She's like my own little sister. I'm just saying: keep her away from the creeps."

"Like you two?" I slap both of their heads in turn.

Boulder laughs. "Exactly! Remember when Sean's sister started to fill out?"

"Keep it to yourself, Boulder." It's rare to see Sean so serious.

"Come on, Sean. She's safe now that she's in college."

"She's family. Do I tell you your mom wears her gym clothes too tight? I mean, really tight?"

"Dude…" Boulder says.

Sean keeps going, "Seriously, sometimes I need to look away. Like, I force myself to make eye contact with her the whole time."

Boulder growls. "Okay, no need to go there. Somebody can get hurt, you know?"

***

"Okay, you guys stay here." Boulder wags his finger at us.

Since he looks older, he'll try to secure the alcohol for the party. It usually takes him three to five tries to find an unsuspecting—or irresponsible—convenience store attendant.

Once he's gone, Sean turns to me. "Are the Weird Sisters coming?"

"I think so. It was Greta's idea, after all."

"Do they know if the other girls in school are game?"

"From what Greta told Skye, the buzz in Fremont is high. They may hate us, but a party is a party."

Sean laughs. "Boulder's parties are legendary."

"Yeah, but he's putting a lot of thought into this one. He's pumped. He was talking about hiring a DJ. He needs this."

"What do you mean?"

"Can you imagine how it must feel for Boulder? He was the star of our team—and he played defense. People came to games just to watch him play. Then he screwed up by getting himself suspended. The Greenwood students were angry because now the team sucks, and the players were mad because they have no chance and no one cares to watch them. He went from the most popular to being a pariah. Two different schools hate him!"

Sean's laugh lines vanish. "Did he tell you this?"

"Are you kidding? He doesn't talk. Does he talk to you?"

"No," Sean says.

I shake my head. "It's the same thing when he lost the scholarship. Dude won't open up."

I see Boulder coming back and tap Sean on the shoulder to warn him.

"Empty hands, big guy?" Sean asks.

"Let's hit the Arco in Shoreline," Boulder answers in a gruff tone.

***

We leave the liquor at Sean's house. Boulder's parents already know all the hiding places their son uses in their house, so the beverages will be safer at Sean's. Boulder is going to pick them up on the day of the party.

When Boulder drives me back home, the earlier conversation with Sean is still in my mind.

"So Boulder, why are you throwing the party again?"

He drives with one hand. His left arm is perched on the driver's windowsill. The freezing wind coming through the opened window makes the car a rolling fridge, but Boulder has a Mustang, and he'll drive it with the windows rolled down, weather be damned.

"What do you mean?"

"Fremont High is not exactly a welcoming place."

"That's my reason. For better or worse, we'll be stuck there for a while. I just want my life to be easier. All of our lives."

He honks at the car ahead of us, whose driver didn't notice the light changing to green.

"Are you okay?"

Boulder looks at me, puzzled. "What?"

Damn, this is hard. "How are you, Boulder?"

"Dude, what are you talking about?"

"I'm just asking you how you are feeling. You know, the football, the scholarship, and all that stuff."

"Damn, D, are you trying to analyze me?"

Thickheaded Boulder. Where's a Truth potion when you need one? "I'm just worried about you. I know what you're going through, man."

"The hell you do!" His expression darkens. "Seriously. Shut. Up. Mind your own business, or I'll go nuclear on your ass."

"I'm trying to help," I mumble.

"You can help by dropping it," he mumbles back.

I throw my hands up. "You suck, you know that?"

He shakes his head. "You are spending too much time with the missus and the Weird Sisters. I think her hormones are passing on to you."

"Ha, ha."

"Maybe you should request to use the women's locker room at Fremont."

"Screw you," I say, looking out of my window.

"See? You're so sensitive. I thought having a girl would make you manlier, not wussier."

"Dude, if you weren't driving, I would punch you."

"Yeah, *that's* what's stopping you, little man."

We mercifully arrive at my house. I leave the car, slamming the door on my way out.

"Really? Storming out, Barbie?" Boulder yells. "Go knit with your girlfriends!"

Chapter 21: Skye

Greta drives Yara and me to Boulder's party. The three of us trapped in a car is uncomfortable for all: we can sense one another's energy. As we approach the house, the scene reminds me of a concert entrance. Greenwood's narrow streets, already crowded by residents' cars, cannot handle the influx of partygoers. We go around the block. The roads around his house have cars parked so close their bumpers touch. A couple of guys are reading the public parking rules.

"Park in any spot," Yara tells Greta. "They don't charge after six."

Greta can't find a space, so she leaves the car in the parking lot of a grocery store. "I'll have to move it later so they don't tow it."

We walk to Boulder's. I have only been there once for a barbecue, weeks ago. The windows, previously damaged by the earthquake, are fixed, and the house, bright with party lights, feels bigger this time.

Drake is waiting for me at the front of the house. He waves, approaches, and gives me a kiss. When we disentangle, I glance at Yara and see her cheeks flushing.

"Big party. Do his parents have a clue?" Greta asks Drake.

"He actually has their blessing," Drake says. "They are going to have a night out and sleep at a fancy hotel downtown." He shakes his head. "Boulder is very persuasive."

"Oh, yeah, he is," Greta says. I look at her, puzzled.

"Priscilla is already inside," Drake tells me. "She was looking for you."

"I'll find her." But then the thought of leaving him with Yara makes me uneasy. I grab him by the scruff of his shirt and pull him to me. I plant a passionate kiss on his lips that lasts too long. Having marked my territory, I make my way into the house, not bothering to look back at any of them.

A guy by the door shakes a hemp cloth bag in front of me. "Keys?" He wears a white cowboy hat with a scribbled note saying "Keymaster!!" pinned on it.

"I didn't drive."

He looks at me suspiciously. "Who drove you?"

"Greta."

He lowers the bag and motions for me to enter. The party is going on strong. No seats are available, and a few girls are already seated on their boyfriends' laps. Daft Punk is playing loudly on the speakers. Red plastic cups cover the mantel and the windowsills.

I find Priscilla on the deck. She's alone and holding a Jamba Juice cup.

"Hey, Pri," I yell. The music is louder here.

Pri doesn't wave or smile. She just glances at a guy with a goatee behind a table with speakers. She points to her ear and then across the backyard.

I nod and follow her. She is way too serious.

When we're away from the speakers, I ask, "Is that the DJ?"

"Yep. Don't know why we need one. An iPod with a decent playlist would do." She takes a sip.

She's acting weird tonight. "Hey, nice outfit," I say, trying to make her loosen up.

"Thanks," she says automatically.

"Pri. Is anything wrong?"

She stares at me and says, "I don't know, Skye. Is it?"

"What do you mean?"

Her stare lasts longer this time. "You don't even know, do you?" She scoffs.

"Pri, just talk to me. What's going on?"

"I expected you'd spend more time with Drake. But I also expected more of you. What's up with the Weird Sisters and you? Listen, I'm not trying to go all Single White Female on you, but I've seen this before. So-called friends who jump ship—"

"Hold on! 'So-called' friends? Is that supposed to be me?"

"What do you think? You don't call. We never talk. We don't go out anymore. When you need a lift, you don't even think of me."

Oh, so that's it. "Pri, it's not like that."

"Really? So what's it like, then?"

I have no answer. I can't tell her Greta, Yara, and I are Sisters. And I cannot think of any other reason why I'd be connected with them, to be honest.

"I was just trying to make friends," I say. It's lame, and we both know it.

Her disappointed eyes zero in on me. "You don't need to ditch your old ones to do that."

"I didn't!"

"Look, Skye. I was alone before you arrived. I thought you and I were true—Oh, great!" She stops herself, looking past me. I glance over my shoulder.

"Hey, girlfriends," Greta says. "Refreshments?" She's holding two red cups.

Pri's expression turns dark for good. She pushes past me and bumps Greta on her way.

The drink spills on Greta, but that's not what worries her. "What did I do? Did I piss her off?"

"No. I did."

Priscilla disappears to the other side of the backyard.

Chapter 22: Drake

Boulder is holding court in the back. When he sees me, he excuses himself and points to the backyard.

"Welcome to Boulder's abode! Where all hours are happy!"

Despite his words, he is serious. We sit by the tree stumps around the fire pit. We're away from people, and I wonder what his weird expression means.

He asks, "Where's the fiancée?"

"With her girlfriends, I guess."

"Congrats on the wedding, D-Man. But it's not about getting the girl; it's about keeping her."

"Aren't you deep this evening, Boulder? And you've told me that already."

"I mean it. Take me, for example. I got Priscilla—"

"*Everybody* got Priscilla, big guy. You're not together. Sorry. I don't know what's gotten into me." I'm still pissed that Boulder dissed me earlier.

Boulder growls. "That's not cool."

"I know. That was uncalled for. I should keep my mouth shut."

"No, man, that's okay." He relaxes. "Didn't you say you wanted to talk? This is me talking."

"Are you already drunk?" I ask. He's not slurring words, but still.

"What does it matter? I'm trying to tell you: I got her. As in, I *get* her. I understand how she thinks. We have—had—a connection. It was a thing."

"A thing?"

"Yeah, a thing. Don't look at me like that; you know exactly what I'm talking about. But she got scared."

A loud curse cuts through the music and chatter. We both look. Two guys start a shoving match by the fence. Nobody tries to prevent it, and they end up stopping themselves.

I turn to Boulder. "So what are you saying?"

"What I'm saying is…"

"Is…?"

"People."

"People?"

"People know me, D. They come to talk. They laugh—maybe with me, maybe at me. We hang out. But they don't care about me. People don't love me."

I say the only possible thing I can. "I love you, man."

He doesn't laugh. "Well, you're not really my type. Thanks, anyway. You and Sean are solid. But…" He gestures aimlessly.

I try to encourage him to keep talking. "But?" I wait for him to finish his thought, but he doesn't. I know he wants to, so I ask, "Who do you want to love you, big man? People? The school? The city of Seattle? A girl? Any girl? Or Priscilla, specifically?"

He eyes me for long time with a blank expression. He is pondering if he should tell me his big secret, but he doesn't remember he already did a couple of months ago. Under a Truth potion concocted by Skye.

"I…love that girl," he whispers.

He looks away with a glassy stare. His shoulders sag. "She gets me. We are alike. And that's why it will never work out. We don't stay attached for too long. We're two sluts." Boulder swallows hard. "Why are we like that? Why do I have to have all the girls?"

Priscilla shows up behind him, not ten feet away from us. Her face is severe, her eyes narrowed.

Before I can warn him, Boulder rambles on. "And why is Pri such a slut? Does she have to give it away to every guy she meets?" Boulder's rant comes out a little louder than he expected, and, as always, his voice carries. His red eyes are still oblivious to her presence.

Priscilla becomes livid. "You scumbag!"

He turns, surprised, and immediately grasps the situation. He rises, startled. "No, Priscilla, I was telling him—"

She steps forward, all rage and menace, and pokes Boulder in the chest. "I know *exactly* what you guys say about me. All of you. But I thought you respected me."

"Pri," I say.

"You shut up, too," she yells at me.

"I do respect you," Boulder says in a meek voice. I've never seen him so helpless.

"How? How in the world is that respect? You make fun of my boobs!"

"What? It's just a joke, Pri."

"It's not a joke to me, is it? I'm a person, you moron. And you tell everybody I'm a slut!" Priscilla doesn't care who hears it.

Boulder shakes his head. "I've never said that."

Her eyes bulge. "You just did!"

"You didn't hear it all. I was just telling him—"

"Screw you! You said to me once that you cared about me. Is that how you care for me?" She makes a dismissive gesture, almost like a slap on the air. "Forget it. I thought we at least were friends." Priscilla looks him in the eye and says deliberately, "Never talk to me again."

She walks away. Boulder and I—and a few partygoers—are still stunned. We'd normally hear catcalls and jokes at this point, but the fallout is too dark to go there.

Boulder slowly puts his cup on the tree stump next to him. He sits down and props his elbows on his knees. His fingertips press his temples.

We spend a few minutes like that. I have no idea what to say. But I think about it, and there's really only one thing I can do. "Go talk to her," I say. "Now."

He has a blank expression. "Let her cool off."

"*Now*, dude."

Chapter 23: Skye

Greta follows me back inside Boulder's house. I keep looking for Priscilla while trying to avoid my noisy new friends. We get to the living room and find Yara furiously texting someone. I wish Pri were a witch, so I could sense her energy and track her down. Instead, I have the Weird Sisters' signatures overwhelming my senses.

I leave the party for a while and find her car outside, around the corner. I'm glad she is not gone. I need to talk to her—even though I have no idea what to say. I get back and join Greta and Yara by the entrance.

"Any sign of her?"

"No," Greta says. Yara doesn't even acknowledge me.

We hear Sean's unmistakable voice yelling, "Dude, are you trying to inhale her?"

The two of us turn to his direction. Yara raises her eyes temporarily—but her fingers don't stop working. Sean is laughing and pointing to a couple making out on the sofa. For once, Sean is right: the junior couple is sharing a slobbery kiss. They finally stop and stare at Sean. The guy's face is redder than the girl's.

"Where did you learn to kiss? Do you guys need a bib?" The smirk on Sean's face stretches for miles.

"Dude, that's how we kiss," the boy says, not intimidated. "Don't be a creep."

Sean laughs. "You are doing it wrong! Here, allow me to explain."

"Hey," the guy rises.

"No, not with her. Chill out." Sean pats the guy on the shoulder, motioning him to sit down. Then he looks around the room. "A volunteer? I need a volunteer!"

Half the room is paying attention to Sean now. He relishes it.

Greta whispers, "That's an interesting proposition."

Priscilla barges through the French doors, coming back from the backyard. Her face is a bright shade of pink. She stops by a table, grabs a red plastic cup sitting there, and downs its contents. She makes a face, but gets hold of another cup.

Greta notices it too. "What's up with her?"

"Something's wrong," I say. Still, I hesitate to talk to her so soon.

A guy approaches Priscilla. She says something to him. The guy backs off, a surprised expression on his face.

"Hey, Pri! Come on over," Sean yells.

She waves at Sean, but she shakes her head.

"Come on!"

Many pairs of eyes are trained on her now, and Pri, still shaking her head, crosses the dining room and approaches Sean. "What?"

"We need to teach those two freshmen how to kiss."

She rolls her eyes. "I'm not kissing him."

"Me neither. *You*," he says, pointing to her, "are kissing *me*." He points to himself.

"The hell I am! Is that what I am to you?"

Sean's smile vanishes. He looks confused. "What do you mean? Just a little kiss. For fun. It's a public service, really."

Priscilla is not sold. "And you decided to ask the slut?"

He is taken aback. And a little offended. "No, I thought about asking my *friend*."

People around them are uncomfortable now. I finally decide to move toward Pri. When I get close, I hear her saying, "Sean…"

"It was just a joke. It's ruined now."

"Come on, girl!" a blonde girl shouts. "He's begging!"

Priscilla looks around. Most of the room is staring at her now. "What the hell." Priscilla puts her hand on Sean's face and kisses him on the lips.

Whistles swirl around the room. Then we hear glass breaking.

I can't see what happened. Too many party guests are in front of me, but some of them are gasping by the French doors.

"Dude, you're bleeding!" Drake's voice comes from the same direction. Then I see my boyfriend making his way through the throng. I move to meet him halfway.

"What?" I ask.

"Boulder just punched the glass door. Help me get some towels."

I follow him into the powder room while we hear some commotion in the living room.

When we come back with the towels, Greta intercepts us. "Boulder just left."

Drake and I go outside, but we can't find him. Then we hear an engine roaring and the screech of tires. A yellow blur appears on the street, and soon it's gone.

"Did he take off?" Drake asks. He turns and runs inside the house. His eyes search the room quickly.

"What's going on?" I ask him.

He moves to the next room and answers me without slowing down. "Boulder saw Pri and Sean." Drake is laser-focused. He gets close to the guy with the cowboy hat and grabs him by the collar. "Did you give him his keys?"

"Drake!" I try to pull him away but he doesn't even notice me.

"No. Nobody asked for keys yet. It's early," the guy says. He's taller than Drake, but scared. "Let me go."

"You're the keymaster! Boulder's drunk as hell! How can you give him the keys?"

"He lives here! He never crossed the front door. He never gave me keys to keep."

Drake releases the guy, not bothering to apologize.

"Are you going after him?" I ask.

Drake snaps at me, "He's in a sports car! What am I going to do, chase him? I have no idea where he went." He gets his phone and tries to find his way outside. Again, I follow him.

Someone grabs my arm. It's Pri. Sean is right beside her. They join us, and we all end up on the front lawn, looking at the street. Drake steps away from us, ear glued to his cell.

Priscilla asks me, "What's going on?"

"He saw you two kissing. He's angry. And drunk."

Her eyes go big, and her face is ashen.

Sean looks puzzled. "So what? He's not jealous, is he?"

"He likes her. As in, he *really* likes her," I try to explain.

Sean doesn't buy it. "No, no. He *had* a crush. Had. He's over her now." Then he turns to Priscilla. "Sorry, Pri."

Priscilla stares at me. "What is it, Skye? Does he like me or what?"

Drake answers it for me. "Boulder is in love with you, idiot! He was just telling me when you crushed him. And then you two dumbasses had to put on a little show for him."

I touch Drake's arm and try to use a soothing tone. "Did you talk to him?"

"No, Boulder didn't answer." Drake looks down and nods toward the ground. "Blood."

I look at the concrete driveway. A trail of sprinkled droplets of blood leads to the parkway.

Drake kicks a can and tries his cell again.

"I didn't know," Sean mumbles.

"Boulder?" Drake speaks into his cell. "Where are you, man?" He beckons to me and puts the cell close to my ear too.

"She stomped on my heart, D-Man…" Boulder's crying.

Drake looks at me with worried eyes. His voice strains to sound calm. "It was nothing. A lame joke. A party game. Where are you?"

Boulder doesn't answer at first. Then we hear, "I don't…have nothing."

"Come on, man, you're not making sense. Tell me where you are, and I'll meet you."

On the phone, the horn of a passing car startles us.

"Dude, are you still driving? Pull over, now," Drake says. His face, his tone: he is terrified. "Come on, stop the car. I'm picking you up, and we can talk."

A loud screech of tires.

Then we hear Boulder's voice cracking on the phone. "So close…"

"Boulder, pull over right now!"

A horn honks again, and then we hear a cry, and then a loud, garbled noise. It sounds like metal grinding and glass shattering. Then the horn once more, only this time, it doesn't stop.

It never stops.

Chapter 24: Drake

Boulder is critical. Like, in a coma, breathing through respirators, critical.

I was talking to him a few hours ago. He was opening up, maybe for the first time in his life. I know he never spoke to Sean so candidly.

Sean. He's taking the news worse than anyone. He cannot stop pacing the room, running his hands through his hair, and biting his knuckles.

Priscilla has cried herself out. She just stares numbly at the wall. Skye has her arms around her, but Pri doesn't seem to notice it.

Sean continues his restless routine. He looks like he's having a panic attack. They just gave Boulder's mother a sedative. Maybe I should ask for some for Sean, too.

I'm trying to come to terms with the situation. I'm on the verge of losing my best friend.

Being back in a hospital is torture. I'm starting to hate these places with a passion.

Something comes over me, and I punch the wall.

A nurse comes over and whispers, "Please don't do that. It upsets everyone. Are you hurt?"

I shake my head. The truth is, my hand is on fire. Something may be broken.

The nurse casts a long glance at me, but leaves.

Skye comes over. "Is your hand okay?"

"Yes," I say, gritting my teeth. The throbbing pain is intense, but I welcome it. It distracts me from everybody else's pain.

"I'm so sorry about Boulder." Skye hugs me.

With my head buried in her hair, I say in a low voice, "I've been so worried about witches and magic hurting one of you that I've never thought... I've never expected that *life* would end up screwing us."

She runs her fingers through my hair. "Me neither."

"Sorry I snapped at you."

"No worries."

We keep hugging, not uttering another word.

It's going to be a long night.

***

The next day, the doctors finally allow visits. We're given a few pointers: we can only be there for a short while, no more than two at a time. They warn us to not be distressed by his condition. Boulder's injuries are mostly internal, but the stitches on his face and arms might upset a visitor.

"Can we talk to him?" I ask.

"Sure," the doctor says. "Please do."

While Boulder's parents go in, I ask Priscilla, "Do you want to come with me?"

She shakes her head. "I'll go tomorrow, by myself."

"I'll go with you," Sean says.

Boulder's parents come back. His mother, Diana, has her head buried in her husband's chest. Jeff, a mountain of a man, has the distant, unfocused stare of someone beaten.

I look away. I don't want to intrude on their pain.

Everybody feels guilty about Boulder: me, Sean, Pri, his parents for giving him permission to have the party. I bet even the keymaster feels rotten.

When it's our turn, we cross the double automatic doors and enter a world of machines humming and whiteness. It feels like heaven's waiting room. I shake off the thought.

We find Boulder's room. Seeing him, even with all the warnings, is still a shock. His eyes are closed. A tube goes into his mouth, and another into his nose. His arm is connected to the IV.

Sean just stares at him, his lips quivering.

Boulder's face is pale, making the wounds, red and black, even more distinctive. He looks lifeless. He, who was so much larger than life.

Is, Drake. Not *was*. Is.

He's smaller, somehow. Not only smaller. Small. Fragile, weak. I'd never thought someone would use these words to describe Boulder.

I can't stand staring at him. I look out of the window. On the streets, lights move. Cars move, people move. How can they keep moving as if nothing had happened? Don't they know Boulder is fighting for his life?

The never-ending rain streaks the window. The steady beep, beep of the machines unnerves me. I take short breaths. I need to do something.

"Hey, big man." My voice sounds different. Alien. "Can you hear me?" Some part of me expects him to open his eyes right away. But he doesn't.

"Listen. Everything's fixed now. You can come back. We're

waiting for you."

Sean nods and moves to grasp Boulder's forearm in a brotherly gesture.

I just can't make myself touch him. It would make it real. As long as it feels like a dream, it's going to be all right. I can wake up, and everything will be fine.

Sean turns to me. "Is it okay if I talk to him alone?"

"Of course." To Boulder, I say, "Hang in there, big man."

I leave my best friends alone.

Chapter 25: Skye

Night has fallen a long time ago. The quietness of the hospital is almost eerie.

Earlier tonight, Sean's parents and Drake's father came to check on Jeff and Diana. Fremont's principal and Greenwood's football coach visited, and a bunch of students from both schools stopped by or called. The Weird Sisters came, and Greta wept in a corner.

Now most of them have gone home. In the ICU waiting room, Priscilla and I stayed. In silence. Jeff sits on the other side of the large room, staring at the wall. Diana and a friend of hers went downstairs to the cafeteria to bring Jeff something to eat.

I'm relieved that Brianna is in another hospital, in another ICU. It would be awkward to explain my presence (and Greta's and Yara's) to the Sisters guarding Brianna. Not to mention I'd feel suffocated by so many energy signatures in one place.

Priscilla hasn't talked since she saw Boulder this afternoon. I don't know what to say to her. I'm starving, and I'm sure Priscilla must be too. We haven't slept for a long time either. But none of this matters to me. I just want to make sure she's well.

But she doesn't look well.

At first, the staff would ask us if we needed something and made sure we knew visiting time was over. Now the nurses come and go, barely looking at us. Jeff remains undisturbed as well. Maybe they realize we need space. They must have seen this many times before.

After half an hour, Priscilla stands up and walks into the hallway, away from the waiting room. There she finds another waiting area. She sits down on a couch. I walk behind her and sit by her side.

She rests her head on my shoulder. In a tentative gesture, I brush her hair with my fingers, like Mum used to do to me when I was sick or sad. Priscilla doesn't complain, so I keep doing it.

But I can hear her breathing harder and harder, and after a few minutes a sob escapes her.

"He'll...die. And it's my fault."

"Oh, no, Pri. That's not true!"

She buries her head in my chest. "It is. He saw us. Sean and me."

"It was an accident."

"He saw us. And...I wanted him to see." She cries freely now, and I let her.

"Pri..."

"I did! I wanted to hurt him. And I have no idea why."

I try to choose my words carefully. "Of course you do, Pri. You like him."

Her sobs stop at last. She finally raises her head and faces me, tears streaking down her face. "I hurt him because I like him? That's not how it works."

I remove a strand of hair stuck to her cheek. "That's exactly how it works, Pri. He pissed you off. You wanted to piss him off right back. Because you care."

She just stares at me. Her crying comes back, softer this time.

"He likes you too, you know?" I say.

Her nod is so subtle I almost miss it. "Skye, this is no better. Did

I play with his feelings? Is that why he is there now?"

"No, no. Stop blaming yourself. Boulder is great, but he's unpredictable too. He overreacted, as always. It was an accident."

"That I caused."

"No!" My voice is louder than hospital etiquette allows. I whisper to her. "Look at me. Repeat: it was an accident."

She shakes her head. Pri's face is naked. No eye shadow, eyeliner, lipstick, mascara. Maybe I'm seeing her as Drake saw me when Jane stole my Allure: still herself, but reduced to her essence. Sometimes we hide behind masks, clothes, and attitudes; other times we conceal emotions. Priscilla today looks genuine in appearance and behavior. I like this truer version of her. Even though she's hurting.

"Say it," I whisper, but my tone is stern.

"It was an accident," she says, looking guilty for having said it.

"There. It'll pass. He likes you, and you like him. When he gets out, you can bicker or you can date. Or both."

"If—"

"*When* he gets out. I'm not just saying it. He's the strongest guy I know," I say.

She nods. It's a lie, but at this moment we both need to believe it.

I offer her a box of tissues from the side table.

Priscilla wipes her face. Her breathing is steadier now. "Maybe I knew it; I just didn't want to admit it."

"He gave you very non-subtle hints." My tone is lighter.

"True. Subtlety is not his strength. I just didn't want to mess it up. Do you know how sometimes…the possibility is better than the real thing?"

"What do you mean?"

Her hands make a helpless gesture. "If we tried to date and we screwed it up—that'd be gone. I preferred not to know. Do you understand?"

"I do," I say. I really do.

"I was too hard on him."

"No. You did what you thought was right. You were true to yourself. At the spa, you said to me you didn't want to be attached, remember? That's the real you. Don't apologize for being yourself."

After a while, she goes to the restroom. She comes back with a clean face and red but calm eyes. She sits by my side.

"Thanks," she says.

I shrug.

"No, I mean it. To listen to me like that—"

"Come on, you were there for me when I was humiliated at school, when Mum had the heart attack, when I screwed up with Drake... I didn't want anything bad to happen to you. But in a way I'm glad I can pay you back."

She says, "You do have much more drama in your life, don't you?"

I'm glad to see her out of her funk. "Want to go home now?"

"Can we stay just for a little while? I'm too tired to drive."

She leans her head on my shoulder again. I go back to brushing her hair with my fingers. My eyes are heavy. Soon she's breathing deeply.

I wake up a little after four in the morning. I make a pillow with my jacket and let Priscilla's head slide over it. I find a comfortable chair and go back to sleep.

***

"But Drake, I want to stay," I plead.

He shakes his head. "Boulder's condition hasn't changed for a week. You've been here with me—"

"And me," Priscilla interrupts.

"—every day," Drake finishes. "I mean, what's the point in Pri and I taking turns if you stay with all of us? *You* are not taking a break. It's not fair."

"Come on, that's the least I can do. Boulder and I are not close, but he's my friend too."

Pri puts her hand on my shoulder. "We're here. His parents too. And Sean. You've been doing enough. More than enough. I wish Boulder could see you." Her mouth smiles, but her eyes don't follow suit. She struggles to contain tears.

"Do me a favor," I say. "You tell him that when he wakes up. I want all the credit."

Priscilla gives a subdued chuckle, more out of sympathy than anything, but at least she doesn't cry again.

Drake squeezes Priscilla's hand. "So it's settled. Pri, Sean, and I will keep coming here after school, and you'll support us from home."

They've been doing it every day. I've heard whispers that they are doing it out of guilt more than anything, but it's just not true. They really love the big guy.

***

Before I leave the hospital, Priscilla grabs me by the arm. "Let's have a coffee," she says.

We buy our beverages at the Starbucks stand next to the cafeteria and walk outside to one of the secluded benches in the garden.

"We didn't finish our conversation at the party," she says.

I'm glad that we have this moment for ourselves. I need to get something off my chest.

"Pri, sorry I haven't been there for you," I say.

She looks at me, puzzled. "You're helping me a lot."

"But before… Pri, with the new school and dating Drake, I was overwhelmed. I'm not looking for excuses. What I'm trying to say is that I should have handled everything better."

"No, no. I get it, really. You have a new boyfriend. That is time-consuming." She tries to smile, but still has a down expression.

"I was just an idiot. I had a boyfriend before, but then I didn't have friends. I messed up. Sorry."

"Well, you did find time for the Weird Sisters." She looks away.

"Oh, Pri. I'm sorry. You're right. I've been an ass, haven't I?"

"What do you see in them, anyway?"

I cannot tell Pri they're witches. I go with yet another lie. "I'm just trying to make friends. I don't have many, you know. And they like the same new age stuff I'm into…"

She takes a deep breath. "Okay."

"I hurt you, and I'm sorry. I'll make up for it, I promise."

She hugs me all of a sudden. "You already did. You got me through these last few days."

"But you just said—"

"I just told you how I felt because we're okay again. You made it okay. I just thought you should know how I was feeling."

"It'll never happen again. We're BFFs, remember?" I hug her tight.

I hear a chuckle. I hope it's a sign that everything will be all right between us.

Chapter 26: Drake

Sean asked me to pick him up. We're going to the hospital to see Boulder.

My guess is that Boulder threw the party because he felt unloved. I wish he could see what's happening: all the calls and visits from students from both schools, the flowers and cards accumulating in his hospital room, the messages of concern and well wishes from everyone. They really care.

I just realized the obvious: Boulder is not with Sean and me. This almost never happens. Actually, I can't remember any other time.

Isn't this strange? Maybe some people are just together because they have friends in common. Maybe Boulder is the glue that keeps Sean and me together. Without the big man, a friendship between Sean and me would never happen.

Our words are scarce. Sean stares out of the window. He's been gloomy and silent since the accident, the opposite of his usual self.

Sean told me he vowed to stop drinking. He still blames himself for Boulder's accident. Himself, and his drinking. And Boulder's drinking.

"I have to stop for gas," I say.

"Sure," he replies, not bothering to look at me. "What's this noise?"

"The engine is shot up. I have no money for a mechanic. Boulder used to fix these things for me."

Sean says nothing.

We park at a mostly empty Arco, and I go inside to pay the cashier. If I had a credit card, I could pay at the pump.

When I get back to the car to fill the tank, a red Dodge truck is parking besides my Volvo, on the other side of the pump. The driver, a bulky, bearded guy in a plaid shirt, leaves the truck and walks to the 7-Eleven store.

A trio of teenage boys at the side of the building motion to him. He walks over to them.

While I pump gas, Sean gets out of the car. He looks straight at the guy and the kids.

The guy inside the store has just paid for a case of Coors.

Sean goes to the back of my car and opens the hatchback.

"What are you looking for, Sean?"

He doesn't answer. Through the window, I see him rummaging around the spare tire section. He gets out the lug-nut wrench.

"Sean?"

He walks toward the side of the store. The guy is handing the beer case to the group.

My responsible self makes me stop pumping and close the gas tank before I go after my friend. "Sean!" I yell.

The kids and the guy are staring at him now, utterly confused. Sean just keeps walking. When he gets there, he moves fast and swings the wrench at the case with all his strength. The bottles inside shatter with a loud noise.

"Shit!" The kid holding the case drops it and steps back with a terrified look on his face.

While I scramble to get there, Sean proceeds to smash the case in a rage. His face turns red all of a sudden. More glass-breaking sounds and the smell of beer fill the night.

I come from behind and say softly, "Sean, dude. Please stop."

He stops. The kids are scared and about to leave the gas station for good.

The bulky man says, "Are you insane? What's your problem?"

Sean turns and looks the man in the eye. The guy doesn't back off. Uh-oh.

Then Sean runs back to my car.

"Yeah, you'd better," the guy taunts.

But Sean passes my car and goes to the other side of the pump. He climbs the hood of the Dodge truck.

"Hey," the guy yells.

Sean brings the wrench down on the truck's windshield. It shatters, but the pieces hold together.

"Stop it!" The guy dashes to his truck, and I race after him.

Sean doesn't hear him. He keeps hitting it like a madman. The guy gets there quickly, but even being much bigger than Sean, he doesn't try to stop him. Sean jumps off the hood onto the ground.

The guy takes this chance to get closer to Sean. When I realize he's going to clock my friend, I jump in front of him.

"Don't!" I say, pushing him back.

His punch hits my arm. Holy cow, it hurts.

The guy is about to strike Sean this time, but Sean points the wrench at him.

"Back off, or I swear I'll split your head open!" Sean screams. He's bright red, and his eyes bulge. "Back off. Back off!"

The guy stops for a second. "You little shit. I'm calling the police."

Sean growls. "Yeah. You do that. I'll tell them how you bought beer for those kids. And how you just hit my friend. Who's also a minor. Go ahead!"

The guy hesitates.

"Come on," Sean says. "Oh, damn it, I'll do it." Sean gets his cell.

The guy looks at us. "You'll go to juvie."

"Do I look like I care?" Sean yells.

The guy jumps into his truck and drives off, windshield shattered and all. I see his license plate and type it on my cell, just in case.

The station attendant comes out of the store. "Go now before I call the police," he says, more scared than any of us.

"Yeah," Sean says. "I know you saw the kids too. Don't play dumb."

The attendant goes inside, but he doesn't go to the phone. He just stays by the glass door, watching us.

"We...uh...should get out of here," I say.

He stares at me. "You okay?"

"Sure." If my arm wasn't firm from all the swimming, I'd be hurting a lot. I shake it off. "At least I wasn't hit on the head again. What about you?"

"I feel better."

"Did you get it out of your system?"

He smirks a bit. The first semblance of a smile since Boulder's accident.

"Let's get out of here," he says, getting into the car.

We leave the station.

"At least your car is running," Sean says. "This noise worries me."

"As long as it runs, I don't care."

"You always drive with both hands. You grab the wheel really hard." Sean points to my hands.

In response, I relax my grip. "Can you blame me? I almost got beat up."

"No, I mean, you *always* do it. Even before Boulder's accident."

I don't answer. It's probably because I'm concerned about Mona. And my mother. And Skye. And Boulder. And the future. Damn, I need to loosen up. I'm turning into Dad.

My paranoid self checks the rearview mirror for a police car or the truck guy. "Still feeling like going to the hospital?" I ask.

Sean shakes his head. "Not tonight. We've been there every day."

"How is the screenwriting going?"

"I stopped for a while. Sorting things out, you know. Hey, let's watch a dumb movie."

The movie takes our mind off Boulder. But when Jason Statham's cop partner dies, I glance at Sean out of the corner of my eye. He is squeezing his eyes shut and gritting his teeth.

Chapter 27: Skye

I'm checking my collection of herbs when my cell rings.

"Hello?"

"Hi! Skye? This is Liam."

"Who?"

"Liam. We met at the club the other night. We danced."

Only then I recognize his sweet voice. "Oh, yeah. You've got some moves," I say.

He chuckles. "You too."

"Not good ones."

"I'll plead the fifth on that. So what's up with you?"

"Nothing much." It's better than saying *a friend of mine is about to die, and I've been trying to support my bestie and my boyfriend.* People don't want to hear that. "What about you?"

"I've been let down by my wardrobe recently. So you up for some shopping?"

Shopping is my main activity with Priscilla. She's at the hospital right now, and I don't want to go with anyone else. It's like I'm betraying her.

"I'm not much of a shopper. Coffee instead?"

"Sure," he says, but he sounds disappointed. "Should I pick you up now?"

"Could it be around six? I have a thing." Yara and Greta are waiting for me.

"No problem."

"I'll text you the address later."

We say our goodbyes. I feel bad leaving Drake and Priscilla taking turns at the hospital, but they both begged me to leave them. And I feel worse meeting Greta and Yara right after Priscilla told me how she felt about it. But I promised the girls I would show up.

**

Despite my earlier reservations, Yara, Greta, and I are having a good time.

"And this one time," Yara says, "I tried to get out of a speeding ticket. I had a cigarette laced with Forget, and while the cop went to the squad car, I lit up. When he comes back, I blow the smoke right in his face. He takes a step back, and yells at me. I have no idea why it didn't work, so I stick my head out of the car, and blow again. He pulls a taser on me! Almost fires it too. My cig was a regular one!"

"That's horrible, Yara," I say.

"Nah. We worked it out later. Anyway, that's why I couldn't drive for a while."

"What about you, Skye? Any embarrassing moments?" Greta asks.

"Well. Priscilla thought you were hitting on me that night at the club. The first time we met."

Greta laughs. "Me? No, I'm straight. Well, straight-ish. It's hard not to kiss a girl once in a while."

I try to think of a comment, but nothing comes to mind. It's a different experience for me, being around Sisters my own age. I've always been a loner.

Greta says, "Hey, I have news. Look." She stands up, turns around, and lifts her shirt a bit.

"A tribal...lower back tattoo?"

"Call it what it is, Skye: it's a tramp stamp. But don't worry. It's temporary. One of mine, actually. Laced with an Energy potion."

"It looks good. I've always wanted one there, but it's hard to get over the stigma."

"You can have one. The one I told you about. With Dispel."

I'm tempted, but this one is supposed to be for Mona. "Maybe another time."

"Come on!" Greta says. "Imagine your boyfriend's face when he sees it."

Yara's face changes subtly, but she says. "Yeah. Here." She gives me a sheet with the design. It has a plastic cover on one side.

I think about it. I can have fun. I'll need a Dispel in some form anyway when Connor makes me take the Truth potion for the deposition. "Okay," I say.

"Use water to apply it."

Greta goes out to get some water.

"How do you make it?"

"It's pretty simple," Yara says. "I need to print the design, right? So I just added the potion and a special emulsion into an empty printer cartridge. I print the design on the paper, and we're done. It's not topical—it needs to enter your bloodstream, so it's okay to be in contact with your skin. Just don't scratch it before you need it."

Greta is back with a damp hand towel. I turn my back to her, and she applies the tattoo.

"Hey, it's too low," I protest.

"It'll look hot. Trust me," Greta says.

They're so wicked. Between them and Priscilla, I feel like a prude.

I'm amazed by Yara's expertise. I thought it was strange, having her and me, with such unique Charms, in the same city. What are the odds? But it makes sense. The Mothers probably tried to assemble the equivalent of an All-Star team of Sisters here to find the Singularity. Well, an Under-17 All-Star team, but still.

While we wait for the tat to dry, Yara says, "Here, try this." She hands me a purple pill.

"What is it?"

"Just take it. You'll be surprised."

Since she knows her stuff, I decide to go for it. I put the pill in my mouth and swallow it.

"What now?" I ask.

"Give it a minute," Greta says. "So Skye, tell us. How did you find the Singularity?"

"Didn't your coven tell you?"

"They told us the girl, Brianna, goes to Greenwood and that you found her. And that she set the school on fire."

That's interesting. It's funny to see it through their eyes. They know just a small part of the whole story. They don't know about the fire—

All of a sudden, I see an image of Yara and Greta on fire. It's like a vision.

"Whoa!" I blink a few times.

"What?"

"Nothing. Weird flashback."

The two of them exchange a furtive glance. I must look like a fool.

"So tell us!" Greta claps excitedly. "Was it dangerous?"

I never thought of a fake version with all the details. I should've expected a request for a play-by-play eventually. But I give them only the highlights—from the *official* version.

"Yes. When I figured it out, I followed her to the school. She freaked out and set the gym on fire by accident. I escaped and dragged her outside."

I don't tell them about the knife at Mona's throat. Or about saving Brianna and Drake with a commune ritual.

Then it comes again, a swift vision of Greta with her throat *impaled* by a knife.

"No!" I yell without meaning to do it. But Greta is before me, unscathed. Then her face blurs a little.

"What's going on?" I ask.

"You're tripping, Skye. Just relax," Greta says.

"What are you talking about?"

Greta and Yara look at each other.

"What?" I ask. They're hiding something from me.

Yara talks to me. "You took a happy pill. I mean, it's going to make you a bit high—"

"Goddess, Yara! Did you drug me?"

She looks at Greta for support, but Greta doesn't open her mouth. Yara says, "Yours is pretty mild. All the coven girls are doing it."

"I don't care! Is that why I'm hallucinating?"

Greta asks, "What do you see?" She's a mix of concerned and curious.

"How do I stop it?"

Yara is worried too. "You can't. Unless you want to waste the Dispel tattoo on it. It's expensive, and it takes a long time to brew, but if you want to..."

I think about it. No, I'd better save it for when it's really necessary. They don't know it, but I need at least two: one to beat Connor's interview, and one to give to Mona just in case. I am wearing one, and I already gave Mona the other.

"It's okay," I say. "I'll tough it out. I just don't like this sensation."

"You could just wait until the effects pass. Should be a half hour or so."

"I need to go," I try to stand up, but my legs are wobbly.

Yara pleads with me. "Please stay, Skye. Give it a little time, and you'll feel better."

"I *want* to go." It's not only the effects: Yara's brightly painted house makes my head hurt—and the visions worse.

Greta bites her lip. "I can't drive you. I'm high too. Can you call a taxi?"

Ack. I look up the time on my cell. Drake must be home by now, after spending the day at the hospital. And I don't want him to see me like this.

I should call Priscilla, but I'd have to explain to her how I got "accidentally" high without mentioning magic.

The cell dings. Liam texted me. I forgot to tell him the address. Maybe he could pick me up. I don't want to give him Yara's exact address, so I just send him an intersection close to her house.

Chapter 28: Drake

The collection of potions and other witch stuff Skye left is just lying on Mona's desk right before me. Since the only other person who enters this room is Pain, she didn't hide any of the vials, pills, and creams.

I have a decision to make. I need to know more about my mother. Dad won't open up, and we're running out of time.

The bottle labeled "Truth" is on the back row. It has the same purplish color of the one Boulder accidentally drank a while ago. Even though it's not a defensive or harmful potion, Skye left it here, "just in case." Maybe this is the case.

Still feeling guilty, I reach for the bottle.

When Dad comes home, I rush to the kitchen and act like I had just finished preparing a smoothie.

"Hey, Dad! How was your day?"

He drops the laptop case on the sofa. "Eventful. Bad eventful. I'm glad it's over."

"Had dinner yet?"

"No, I'll just fix myself a sandwich."

"Here, grab a smoothie."

Dad looks at the purple-red concoction I'm offering him. "What's this?"

"A mixed berry smoothie. Or you can have mine." I show him a kale smoothie. It's dark green. It looks like I made it out of moss and dirty twigs.

"I'll have the berry one, thanks." He reaches out, smells it, and takes a sip. "Not bad." He takes a full swig and sits at the nook's table. "How is school?"

"Fremont is okay. At least the gang is all there. We miss Boulder though."

"How's he?"

"The same," I say, sitting at the table opposite him. "I went there after school."

"A shame, what happened to that boy. I called his father the other day; he is devastated. I wish I could help." He looks away for a few seconds and shakes his head. "Jeff asked me to tell you that you're a good friend, buddy."

"That's cool."

"You're a stand up guy. You go to school, help with the house, keep an eye on Mona..." His weary expression is improving. "I'm proud of you, Drake."

Uh-oh. The potion is already taking effect. I feel bad, but this is nice to hear.

He goes on. "You should go to college. You have top grades. We can pay for it, you know. Tuition at U-Dub is expensive, but as residents we get a discount. I have a little set aside for that. Maybe a student loan can complement it. We'll figure it out." His eyes glaze. "But it's your decision. I want you to make your own path. I didn't, and sometimes I regret it a little." He takes another sip.

I'm ashamed of my behavior, but I want to know more. When am I going to get another chance to have a frank talk with him? "What would you rather have done?"

He chuckles. "That's the thing. I don't really know. That's why I said I regret it a *little*. I just imagine how things could have been. One thing I wouldn't change is having you and Mona. But the job, the place, and, you know, life… I wonder, 'what if?'"

Here's my cue. "Do you wonder 'what if?' about Mom?"

Dad looks at me. "Yes. That, most of all." He finishes his glass.

I almost choke when the words come out, "Why did she leave, Dad?"

His eyes move to outside the kitchen window. "She didn't love me anymore."

A pang in my chest almost stops me from asking, "How do you know?"

Dad grits his teeth. "She told me. I was shocked. It was sudden. We were living a happy life, as a family. One day, I noticed her getting restless. Different. Two weeks later, she dropped the bomb." He rubs his forehead. "I tried to argue. I asked about the kids. She said she did love you, but she needed to leave." He touches my arm and looks me in the eye. "Never forget this, Drake. She always loved you and Mona."

When he lets go of my arm, I look away. I don't want him to see my watering eyes. But I need to press on. "What else did she say?"

"She told me to always keep an eye on you and Mona. She said you two were special and had potential to be great."

Okay, here's where I trust that he'll forget all about it when the potion effects disperse. "Was Mom a witch, Dad?"

He blinks a few times. "Why do you ask?"

"Was she?"

"I don't know. At times I thought she had a secret. Or maybe a secret life. She always got what she wanted; that part was almost…supernatural. Well, unnatural."

"Was she also, uh, unnaturally beautiful? Or smart? Or athletic?" From what Skye told me, those are the most common Charms.

My father smiles. "In my eyes, yes. Of course. I was in love with her. But no, not really. The only weird thing was that she could make everyone agree with her and give her what she wanted." He snorts. "How do you think she convinced me to let her go?"

I don't know how much longer the potion is going to last. "So do you think she might be a witch?"

"This is ridiculous. But I do. She had something magical about her."

"Where is she now?"

"I don't know," Dad says.

"Guess."

"She didn't have a family. Her parents—your grandparents—passed away a long time ago; I've never met them." He sighs. "She always said she wanted to see the world."

Great. This narrows things down. "Dad. Do you want to see her again?"

He nods. "More than anything."

I lower my head. I wanted the truth. I just didn't realize it would hurt so much. This session is taking a heavy toll—on both of us.

"Well, look at the time!" Dad says in an upbeat voice. "I didn't realize it was so late."

He smiles at me and gets up. "Thanks for the drink, Drake. But it tasted bitter."

Yes, it did.

Chapter 29: Skye

For some reason, Liam's car doesn't match the owner. I don't know what I was expecting, but it certainly wasn't a black Lexus sedan with tinted windows. He parks by the curb, and the passenger's window slides down.

"Taxi for one?" He is showing his winning smile.

"Thanks for picking me up," I say, getting into the car. It's the first time I see his aura; Mona had borrowed my glasses when I went to the club. His aura looks dark. Maybe it's the dim lights on the car.

"My pleasure," he says. "Fasten your seatbelt." He presses a button; my window closes.

"Concerned about my safety?" I giggle.

"No," he says. "Quite the opposite."

I look at him, puzzled.

A piece of cloth covers my face. I struggle and try to get away, but Liam holds my arms in a strong grip while the person behind me presses the cloth against my mouth and nose. I fade into oblivion.

***

My disorientation is a familiar one. Thanks to Jane, I know how waking up from a Sleep potion feels.

The True Sight tingling is abuzz, as if a low electrical current permeates my body.

The intense magical energy and the aftereffects of the Sleep Potion and of whatever Yara drugged me with make me dizzy and confused. I need to focus. I try to recognize the place.

The absence of windows tells me I'm in a basement. It's not a rundown house, but an *eerily* normal one. Except for the metal pole against my back. When I try to get in a better position, the pain in my wrists hints at handcuffs. I don't feel the cold touch of steel handcuffs, though. I use my fingers to find out what is holding me: hard plastic strips.

My heart beats faster. I've been kidnapped. Where's Liam?

"She's awake," says a voice behind me. The noise alerted my captors.

Liam comes into my field of vision, followed by a short, mid-twenties, red-haired woman. He has a bored expression, but she is downright pissed. The magical energy comes from her.

This is not good. My heartbeat is out of control.

My cell was inside my jacket, and I'm not wearing it.

The woman kneels in front of me. "Hello, princess. Yes, you're sensing it right. I'm a Sister too."

"Are you insane? This is a crime. Let me go right now!"

"Of course no one can hear you, so please stop screaming. It's really annoying."

I clench my teeth, trying to take calmer breaths. "Who are you?"

Instead of answering, she turns to Liam. "Get the Truth potion, will you, dear?"

He goes to a table to my left and collects a vial.

"I won't drink it."

The woman turns to me and smiles. She's beautiful. Allure. "You won't need to. You will tell me all I want to know, won't you, princess?"

I feel an urge to tell her anything she asks. Trust. She has a Trust Charm. She must be a Night Witch.

Liam is coming with a vial and a syringe. This must be about the Search.

Yara's tattoo. I can't see what I'm doing, but I make my spine straight to bring my lower back close to the pipe I'm handcuffed to. Without moving my arms, I scratch myself madly on the small of my back over and over again, hoping to break through the tattoo's film.

The pain is almost imperceptible, lost amidst the dull throb of the handcuffs on my wrists and the strong True Sight buzz from having a witch so close. But a warm liquid trickles down my back. The scratches drew blood. The Dispel potion laced into the tattoo should have mixed with my blood. Goddess, please make it so.

Just in time. Liam kneels downs by my side and without uttering a word, plunges the needle into my arm.

I grunt. The room swirls around me. The woman's black-and-white power suit blurs for a second. Oh, Goddess, the tattoo didn't work.

But soon my vision straightens. A light dizziness is still there, though. The Dispel didn't cancel the potion completely.

Liam scoots over in front of me and puts his hand on my face, pulling the skin underneath my eye down. "Her pupils are dilated. She's ready. Remember, start slow."

She kisses him on the cheek. "I've done this before, my sweet little Knowing. And my potion is strong." She switches position and sits cross-legged in front of me. "Are you Skye, daughter of Dame Katherine?"

I nod.

She slaps me.

My face burns, and my heartbeat goes up again. Only I can't show it. She must believe I'm under her potion.

"Why did you do that for?" Liam asks. "She will tell you everything anyway."

"I just felt like it," she snarls. Then she adds with a sweeter voice, "Go make us some coffee, will you, sugar?"

I need to fake it better. I'm glad Liam distracted the woman, giving me time to recover. But now he's gone, and I'm at her mercy.

"I'm Skye," I say meekly.

"Where's Jane?"

I almost betray my surprise. "I don't know."

"What did you do to her?"

"Nothing."

"Is she dead?"

I know what I should say, but I almost blurt out, "No." The potion is strong. The Dispel doesn't work on her Trust Charm. Her Charm and the residual Truth potion make a compelling case for telling her all my secrets. I can't rely on the Dispel alone. I must fight.

She mistakes my hesitation and looks at the vial. She gets the syringe, refills it with the last drops from the vial, and stabs me with the needle again. Lying will be even harder now. She looks at her watch, and then she repeats, "Is Jane dead?"

"I don't know."

"When did you last see her?"

Not in the gym, Skye. Tell her *part* of the truth. "At the hospital. She was unconscious."

"When did you arrive in Seattle?"

"October 21st."

"When did you find the Singularity?"

"November 17th."

"Who is the Singularity?"

Mona! Mona is! No, no. What's her name again? "Brianna."

"How do you know?"

How indeed? Nobody has asked me this before, so I don't have a prepared lie. "The gym. She set the gym on fire."

She leans over, studying my face. "But how *can* you know?"

Think fast, Skye. "I was there."

She's taken aback. "I didn't know that."

Liam comes with two mugs of coffee and gives one to the woman. "Miranda, why don't you try being more conversational? It looks like an interrogation."

She rises, still holding the mug, and puts her hand on his abdomen. "Liam, sugar, I love you very much, but you need to let me do this my way. Okay?" Her hand goes to his back and she pulls him into a kiss. "Would you do that for me?"

He smiles. "Of course."

"Thanks. You can sit in, but let me do the talking." She takes up her position in front of me.

The interruption allowed me to clear my head, calm down, and come up with a story. I'm ready now.

She sips her coffee. "What were you doing at the school?"

"I felt Brianna's energy during the earthquake."

"We all felt the energy then. How could you pinpoint Brianna's location?"

"She lives close to school and to Aunt Gemma's house." My lies need to sound truthful, so I try to sprinkle a few real facts into my story. "There was residual energy after the quake."

She turns to Liam. "I've never heard of 'residual energy'."

Liam shrugs. "You told me the Singularity's energy didn't follow the usual patterns."

Miranda considers this carefully.

During that stoppage, I realize that Jane has never told them about Mona. It's been weeks now, and they don't know. They don't even know that Jane was there. Or that she's still alive. Why? Why hadn't she told them? Maybe she's dead. Or hurt.

Or maybe Jane wants the Singularity's power to herself.

Miranda addresses me again. "Then what?"

"We followed her to school, and maybe she saw us. Drake and I."

The worst part is having to make a benign face while she interrogates me. I can't show my contempt, my fear, or my discomfort with the handcuffs. The Truth potion drinker is docile and malleable.

"Is Drake your boyfriend?"

"Yes." I show her a puppy-love smile to sell my acting.

"Is he a Knowing?"

Crap. "Y-yes."

Her eyes narrow. "Why did you hesitate?"

"Because… Because… I broke the Veil!"

She relaxes and smirks. "Yes, you did. So you followed Brianna, and…?"

"And she saw us. I was looking for the Singularity. I couldn't just let her go. So we chased her into the gym. She was terrified. She had just caused the earthquake. She freaked out and set the place on fire. We rescued her and called 911."

"The call came from *her* cell."

How do they know that? "Yes. We got it from her. I didn't want

149

to be involved with the fire and the investigation."

Miranda's fingers drum on the floor. She gets up and approaches Liam. "This was useless." She drinks more coffee and rests the mug on the table.

"Something's wrong about Brianna being the Singularity." He faces me and asks, "How could Jane be so close and not know?"

I lied about that before, so I do have an answer. "I think Brianna wanted to get close to a Sister so she could learn how to control her magic. She doesn't come from a coven family. When Jane came to Greenwood, Brianna sensed a Sister's energy and got attached to Jane."

Liam nods. "It makes sense."

Miranda snorts. "Yeah, the princess is smart. I just can't believe Jane got played."

He points his mug at her. "Well, she did get played by your coven."

"Did she? Then why hasn't she come back?" She turns to me. "Why, princess?"

"I don't know."

"Guess!" Miranda commands.

"She wanted to steal the Singularity's power for herself?" I hope they buy it.

Liam is surprised. "How do you know about Jane's Charm?"

"She tried to kill me. She tried to steal my Allure." My hatred is genuine.

Liam raises his eyebrows. "That sounds like Jane."

"If Jane had stolen the princess' Allure, maybe it had fixed her horse face. So maybe Jane was playing *us*, huh?"

"Come on, we knew she could try that."

Miranda nods. "Yep. Now we have to kill Jason."

Liam makes a face. "Do we? It's always a hassle. And a mess. Let's keep him until Jane resurfaces. We can still use him."

"What difference does it make? We need to get rid of her too."

Her, I realize with terror, is me. Miranda is pointing at me.

Chapter 30: Drake

Boulder is leaving us. I know it. I can feel it.

The way the accident happened weighs on me. I keep replaying the night in my head. If Priscilla hadn't heard Boulder's comments. If Sean hadn't asked her—or if she had refused, or if Boulder hadn't seen them.

And all the things I could have done—or not done. Not forcing him to open up. Not telling him to talk to Pri right away. Not leaving his side to get a towel. Making sure he didn't have his car keys.

I once read that for a catastrophic event to happen, many things have to go wrong at the same time. The book said that in a particular nuclear plant incident, twenty-two different systems and safety measures failed in succession.

It's cruel that Boulder had such bad luck—on top of his ongoing bad luck streak: being hated by two schools and losing everything he truly wanted—football, college, Priscilla.

Seeing him like this is the worst. I wish I could do something. I wish I were a doctor. A great doctor. A doctor with super powers.

Dumb.

Dumb, stupid Drake. I don't have super powers, but Mona does. She may even have that Healing Charm that Skye mentioned. I mean, she helped Brianna and me after the fire.

I need to know how she would feel about it. I go upstairs and knock on her door.

"What?"

I open the door. "I think you mean, 'come in'."

"You think wrong." Mona is seated on her bed, a couple of upturned books around her, a highlighter pen in her hand.

"What's this annoying music?"

"It's Thursday."

"No, it's Wednesday."

"Thursday, the band, you geek. And they're great."

"Mona, have you thought about what you're doing with your magic?"

Her face loses its color. "What?"

"You're this super-girl now. What are you doing with your powers?"

"Damn, Drake. That's a hell of a thing to spring on me."

"Come on, you must have thought about that."

She scratches her head. "I did. I don't think it's an accident."

I walk up to her and sit on the bed. "What do you mean?"

Mona props herself up on the bed so her spine is straighter. "If I have this, I should use it, right? Not for me. For people. What? You're smiling like an idiot."

"That's good to know."

"What did you expect of me, Drake? That I would use it for make money or something?"

"No, no. What you said is *exactly* what I expected to hear from you."

"Oh." She looks embarrassed. "Then it's okay, I guess. But it's pointless, right? I can't use the magic without triggering a witch tornado warning. If we don't solve that, all this power will be for nothing."

"We'll figure it out, Mona. Don't worry."

"Is that it? That's all you came here to ask me?"

"Yep."

She rolls her eyes. "You're so weird! Get out of my room."

After I leave her bedroom, I walk down the stairs, beaming. I need a plan. We might be able to help Boulder.

Chapter 31: Skye

Liam hesitates to kill me. "I prefer not to do that. I see no point in hiring a witch assassin if we will end up doing the killing ourselves. Maybe we should have Scythe go after Jane instead."

Miranda ponders that. "Jane is not important. The Singularity is."

"Anyway, I think we should spare this one." He points at me. "You told me that when the Truth potion wears off, she won't remember it anyway."

"It doesn't work like that," Miranda says. "The person doesn't remember what she said, but the other memories will be there. She'll know that *something* happened. She will have a bad feeling about you and might remember you're not her friend. But the main reason is that there's a slight chance she'll remember my face and this place. We can't afford that."

"We should've thought of that before bringing her here."

"Oh, I did. But I needed to question her myself. Look at me." She caresses Liam's face. "This is on me, Liam. My coven trusted me with the Search. I tracked down Jane and put her to it. If we don't get the Singularity back, Kendall will have my head. Literally."

"I'm kind of attached to your head," he says.

She stares at him, perplexed. Then she smiles and kisses him. "Me too."

My mind spins everywhere. Even with my brain still muddled by the potion, I need to think. I had a couple of vials in my back pocket, but I can't feel them in my pants anymore. They have taken them. The plastic handcuffs are fastened tight, but they'll have to uncuff me to kill me.

Will they kill me here and dump my body? Maybe they'll take me somewhere else and then kill me there. Grim thoughts or not, I need to consider all possibilities: the cell in the jacket's pocket, their strength versus mine, running through the door.

"Okay, one last thing," Liam says. "She's pretty high profile. She is a heroine to them. Wouldn't that stir things up? They might increase the security around the Brianna girl."

"Well, I also want to kill her because she beat me to the Singularity," Miranda says with venom. "But you're right. Kendall might not like it."

Miranda looks dejected. The prospect of not killing me is hard for her. She paces the room while Liam sips his coffee.

They're discussing my death in a relaxed way, as if they have an unshakeable confidence that nobody is looking for me and that nobody will catch them. I wish they were yelling at me. Their calm is terrifying.

"Damn it!" Miranda snaps. "Let's give her a Forget potion. Then she'll have absolutely no memory."

Liam gets a syringe and approaches me. He sticks the needle into my arm and the potion enters my bloodstream. After he leaves the syringe on the table, he says, "You'll have your revenge, Miranda. Just be patient."

She smiles with malevolence. "No, I don't need to be patient." She approaches and stands in front of me. Miranda raises her foot and kicks me in the face.

I yelp. The back of my head bangs on the metal pole, and the sharp sting under my eye adds to the throbbing pain in the back of my head. I need to lie down. My body slides down to the concrete floor. My arms, still cuffed, twist.

"Let's test the limits of the Allure Charm," Miranda says. Then she stomps on my face.

A cut above my eye starts to bleed. I see Liam rising.

"I'll leave you girls to it." He goes out of the basement and closes the door behind him.

Miranda doesn't turn, doesn't say anything back to him. She just kicks me in the nose.

After a few kicks, I faint.

***

When I regain my bearings, I'm down on the floor of something bumpy. It moves. It's disorienting. I open and shut my eyes quickly. A van. I keep faking I am out.

It isn't easy. I want to moan, to yell, to cry.

My entire head hurts like hell. My face is on fire, covered with something liquid, viscous—it must be a mixture of tears, dirt, and blood. She didn't just break my nose; she destroyed it. I'm using all my strength not to yell. The excruciating pain is like a hot iron poking my brain.

They gave me an injection with Forget potion, but the Dispel took care of it. So far. I hope it holds. Under any other circumstances, I'd want to forget what had happened. But I need to remember. I need to remember all they said. And I need to know who did this to me, so I can get back at them.

A small part of me is actually grateful she only battered my face. I was afraid they would break me, scar me for life, violate me. The Allure might heal that—in time.

And I'm still alive. It's the worst of feelings: being grateful to somebody because they didn't kill you.

Since I don't dare to open my eyes, I can't tell where they've brought me. They think I'm still out while they drag me out of the van. Miranda's energy this close is overwhelming, but I keep my control and don't let my body shake.

The freezing night air doesn't even bother me. It's nothing compared to the pain.

Liam catches me under my arms and carries me, my feet scraping on the ground. It sounds like a gravel path.

Then I feel it. Another signature. Far away, but distinct. Another Sister is nearby, but not close enough to alert Miranda.

"Just leave her behind the bushes. Remember to get all her valuables," Miranda instructs.

Liam proceeds to search my pockets. He also takes his time feeling me up. The bastard.

"Where's her phone?" he asks.

"I got it," Miranda says from a distance. Then I hear a splashing sound. "I mean, the lake's got it now."

He cups his hands over my breasts. I almost give in and punch him.

Liam leaves me and walks away. "A waste of time. We should be worried about Jane," he says to Miranda.

Her voice comes from somewhere close to the van. "I know. Trust me, I'd love to get my hands on Jane. Don't worry, she will come to us. Are you done, sugar? We need to go."

My two captors enter the van and leave in a flash. It's almost as if they weren't here.

I open my eyes but don't move. The energy source is closing fast. It seems I'm in a park. The faint moonlight lets me see the bushes around me. Soft waves are hitting a beach not far away.

Getting to my knees, I try to regain my balance. I look in the direction the energy is coming from, but I can't see her. The low growl of an engine approaching freezes my blood.

Jane has never collected her motorcycle from the impound lot, as far as I know. But she's the only biker Sister I can think of right now.

My muscles ache from the beating and the hours in awkward positions. I'm in no condition to flee. I hope she won't see me, but I know she's coming for me. I need to hide.

I crawl to a line of bushes nearby. The pain in my face makes me dizzy. I try to steady myself, grasping on a branch, only it's too thin to hold my weight, and I almost tumble over.

But I keep going. I can't let her find me.

Stumbling through the vegetation, I reach a clearing. She's close enough to sense me now.

It's over. I stop and turn. My potions are gone; Miranda took them all. My only defense is the Dispel. If it's still active.

The engine stops rumbling nearby. She must be near where the van was. I can hear footsteps on the gravel.

"Skye?" she calls. "It's okay."

I've defeated her before. I can fake that I'm even weaker than I really am, and, when she's close, I'll strike her and make a run for it. It's my only hope: my cell is gone and no one is going to hear me scream. But it's not going to be enough. Jane is stronger and way more athletic than I am, even if I weren't beaten up. She'll catch me.

Now twigs crunch under her boots. She's close. She appears from behind a tree, most of her face hidden by a hoodie. She stays in the shadow.

"You're alive, thank Goddess," she says.

Who does she think she's kidding? Despite my exhaustion, I get up. I make fists and wait for her to get close.

"Did you see a boy in the house?"

"What?" My mind is still addled. "You mean, Liam?"

"No. Younger. Fifteen. Did you?"

"No!" Why am I humoring her? She's trying to distract me.

"Did you hear anything about him? Or the name Jason?"

"Why?"

"Just tell me! Is he still alive?" she asks in an anxious voice.

"Yes. They plan to kill him. I don't know where or who he is."

My answer makes her go quiet. Her hands shake, but she closes them in fists, and the trembling stops. She takes a step toward me. "You look like hell," she says.

I can't help but answer her. "Satisfied?"

"Not really. It's not fun. I should know. Remember these?" She removes the hoodie.

I let out a gasp.

She points to a series of small scars on her cheek. "This is where you broke the glass vial and cut me." Her hand goes to the other side. "And this is what the fire did to the rest of my face."

That side of her face has a depressed lesion. It looks like part of her flesh melted and vanished. The remaining skin is thin, stretched.

A twinge of guilt and a speck of sympathy almost make me forget who she is. That she's here for revenge.

"You tried to kill me. And Mona," I say.

"I was left to die in the gym. You saved Brianna, but not me."

"You were gone!"

She snorts. "Yeah, yeah. Always an excuse. You're so worked up I broke into your house, but you did the same to mine." She points to the cut scars again.

"You've been following me. Here, and at Aurora Park!"

"No, just here. And I wasn't after you, just keeping an eye on Miranda."

I don't know what to say. I just wait for her next move, but she's doing the same. We're at a standoff.

She narrows her eyes and asks, "How did you know I was here? You started to run before you could sense me."

"The bike—"

"Bullshit. I saw you. You looked right at me. What is it? You have a long-range sense? Is that it? That's how you tricked me the other times, isn't it?"

I'm not that strong. In my mind, I have a vision of Jane killing me and stealing my True Sight, then killing Mona and getting all her power. My body trembles. I wish I were tougher.

"You do! That's why they chose you to find the Singularity." She scrutinizes me with even more intensity. "That's perfect, actually. I need your help."

I may have brain damage from the kicks. "What?"

"We're both...scarred. Let's call it even. Look," she says while getting something from her back pocket. Her knife.

"Jane..."

"No, it's okay. See?" She throws it away. "I'm not here to hurt you."

My nerves are frazzled. "Are you insane? Am I supposed to be grateful because you won't kill me?"

She's taken aback. "Neither you nor Mona."

"Wow, thank you for letting me live. What's this sick game you and Miranda are playing? Do you expect me to believe she didn't know about Mona?"

"She didn't. Why would she get you—"

"Yeah, how come you're here just in time to 'help me', huh?" I'm out of it, shouting, crying. The blood and tears make my vision blur.

"Goddess, calm down. I was following them. I'm trying to—"

But I don't listen. I try to go after her. "Go away. Just go! Leave me alone. Get out of my life."

Jane swats my weak slaps away easily, more stunned than afraid. "Okay, okay." She pushes me away. "Get a grip."

I take two steps back, panting.

She walks to her left, picks up her knife, and puts it back in her pocket. Then she gets a small cell from another pocket. "Here," she says. "We'll need to talk, sooner or later. This is a prepaid phone, so the Night covens can't trace it. You can use it to call for help too." She throws it at my feet. It lands with a soft thud on the dirt.

After she leaves, her motorcycle's roar just a faint purr in the distance, I fall to my knees, shaking. I hate myself for some reason. My nails dig deep into my arms, but I don't feel anything.

I could take Miranda's beating; I could take Jane's return from the dead. But not both on the same night. I'm crying angrily—at them, at me. At their cruelty, at my weakness.

I don't know what I'm doing anymore. Worse, I don't understand what's going on.

The tears ebb. The blood on my face is drying. I look at my fingernails and see pieces of skin stuck under them.

Pull yourself together, Skye. You're better than that. Show them.

Chapter 32: Drake

Every time Skye and Mona lock themselves up in my sister's bedroom, an uneasy sensation comes over me. I fear that Mona might share, accidentally or not, some obscure and embarrassing anecdote about my childhood. Or that Skye would let slip any detail of our relationship, which Mona would bring up just to see me squirm.

Mostly, I have the lingering feeling that Mona might blow up our house if she loses control of her magic.

But right now, Mona is alone in her room. She may be talking on the phone with Pain, or reading, or putting on her goth makeup. Or she could be doing spells and putting our lives in danger.

I don't want to think about it. That's why I'm playing Xbox and trying to focus on the game. The new TV is not as big as the one that broke during the earthquake, but the sound is amazing.

The doorbell is still louder than the game, though. I pause my game with reluctance, leaving my virtual squad hanging, and walk to the door.

Yara is there, a lopsided grin on her face.

"Hey," I say. My face must betray my puzzlement.

"Hey, Drake," she says.

A pause. "How are you?"

"I'm good."

"Can I help you?"

"Yeah, I have good news. May I?" She points to my living room.

"I guess. I mean, sure." I open the door all the way and let her in.

"Thanks," she says, scurrying into the house. She sits on the sofa before I have the chance to offer.

I close the door behind her and follow her to the living room. "What's up?" I ask, getting the lounger for myself.

Her smile fades. "Direct, aren't you?"

"Oh, sorry. Do you want something to drink?"

She chuckles. "I'm just messing with you. And yes, can I have a diet soda? I'm thirsty."

We go to the kitchen, and I hand her a soda. "So..."

She takes a sip. "I heard the guys talking about how you used to take pre-calc at Greenwood."

"Yeah. But they don't have it at Fremont."

She plays with the magnets on the fridge. "I know. They don't have chem either, but I got a special waiver to attend Ballard's classes. They have pre-calc and a bunch of accelerated learning classes. That's what I wanted to tell you. You could apply too."

That's interesting. I miss those classes, and they could help me if I eventually decide to go to college. "Do you think the district would approve? We're in the middle of senior year."

"Well, the earthquake messed up everything. They should consider the circumstances, right?"

That could work. "You're right, Yara. I didn't know about it. Thanks."

Her face lights up. "No problem, *gatinho*." She steps toward me.

Instead of asking what the word means, I say, "But you didn't need to come all the way here. You could've just told me at school."

"It's no trouble, Drake. Besides, when do we have the time to be by ourselves at school? I mean, just the two of us."

Uh-oh. I'm getting a vibe. Is Yara flirting? I've been wrong about this before. Like, a million times. A million embarrassing times. At the last party, I thought Priscilla was coming on to me, but she wasn't at all. I'm probably imagining things again.

"Right," I say. "It's cool to hang out outside school."

She nods. Then her back straightens. Her smile is gone, and she's looking at the ceiling. "Is Skye here?" she asks.

"What? No."

"You sure?"

What is that? "I would know, wouldn't I?" Maybe she *is* flirting with me.

"Is Greta?"

"What? No. Why would she?"

Yara pierces me with her eyes. "Who's upstairs?"

"Just my sister."

"Is your sister…a Sister?"

It takes me a while to process her question. When I do, my whole body tenses. Crap. I have no idea what to do.

Yara looks at me with a confused expression. "Skye told us you're a Knowing. I thought you became one because of Skye. I've never imagined your sister was one too."

I jump to my feet. What do I do? Skye would know. I cup my hands in front of my mouth and shout, "Mona, stop what you're doing! Now!"

Yara is startled. She rises and looks up again. "It's gone. How did she do that?"

165

Then, just to make it worse, Mona yells while coming back down, "Hey, dummy. I was busy—" She halts when she sees Yara. "Hi." Mona looks at me with an inquisitive look.

"Hey, Mona. This is Yara. Mona, please go back up and read a book or something. Don't do anything else."

She scoffs. "What are the odds I'll do what you tell me to do?"

"Please?" I plead.

Mona glances at Yara, and something must have clicked in her brain, because she says, "You got it." Mona jogs back upstairs.

"Wait," Yara says, but my sister goes to her bedroom and slams the door. "What just happened?" Yara asks me. "I felt nothing, then one source, then the energy was gone."

I try to salvage the situation, but my attempt is lame. "Skye may have been visiting. She goes in and out through the window. She likes to climb. Rock-climbing."

Yara tilts her head. "If this were true, I'd have felt the energy increasing and decreasing. It doesn't just vanish."

I think fast. "Yara, please hear me out. Sit down."

"Drake, I know Sisters don't work that way."

"Yeah. Mona is not a Sister. It's a secret. But you can't tell anyone. Promise?"

She tilts her head.

Yara is damn smart. I need to fake being smarter. "The truth is…Skye gave Mona a magical amulet." All this time I thought I wasn't a gambler.

"A what?"

"A magical thingie." I make a vague shape with my hands. "I'm not sure what it is. It's Mona's. She doesn't let me near it. It's advanced stuff, apparently. You can deposit your…personal magic?

166

Is that what you call it? You transfer it into a vessel, and it's stored there." I make it up as I go. The problem is, I don't know how to stop it. "When you need it, you can transfer it back to the Sister."

Yara looks past me, in deep thought. "That's not real. That's the stuff of fantasy." Her smile is gone for good now, and it's not sending a postcard.

"No, it's real. Skye told me it's possible. Advanced Craft, remember? That's...that's why she gave it to Mona. So Mona could hold it for Skye. Skye said she'd in trouble with her coven if she were caught with it." I lower my voice. "Skye might have stolen it. Maybe she brought it from England."

It's a huge bluff. It turns out it's so convoluted that Yara is in doubt. "Really?" She looks at me, but I keep my poker face. "I thought amulets only stored a tiny bit of magic, tied with a spell. And that they didn't emanate energy. Are you sure?"

I open my arms. "That's what Skye told me."

"And the energy?"

"I think that when Mona activates it somehow, it releases the energy. Just a little? I wouldn't know."

"That's why you shouted at her to stop it. She could have let it all out."

"Exactly!" She's buying it.

"So is Mona a Knowing too?"

Oh. "That makes sense. I mean, she is."

"How old is she?"

"Just turned fifteen."

Yara raises her eyebrows. "You keep an eye on her, then. She might end up being a Sister, after all."

"I doubt that. But I'll pay attention," I say, trying to relax my voice. "So can you keep the secret? Please?"

"I don't know. I want to know more about it. May I see the amulet?"

"No! That's not right. It's not mine. Come on, Yara. I leveled with you. Please don't tell anyone. Not even Greta."

"I'm not sure about that. I tell Greta almost everything. This is a big favor."

"I know. I'm asking as your friend."

Yara stands up slowly and looks at me. She has a different glint in her eyes. "Maybe you could do me a favor back?" Her voice is low.

"Sure. Anything."

She approaches me. It just takes me a second to realize what she intends to do. Her lips get close to mine, her minty, hot breath inviting in a strange way. She closes her eyes. We stop, frozen. A million thoughts cross my mind in that instant, but when she presses her lips to mine, I don't push her away. It's a chaste kiss. Nevertheless, it makes me warm inside. And guilty as hell.

She pulls back in a slow movement, opens her eyes, and smiles at me. "Now we both have a secret. I'll keep yours if you keep mine."

"Yara, you know I can't do that."

"It's just a kiss, silly. Don't worry. Both secrets are safe."

She caresses my cheek before walking to the door.

"Not even Greta, okay?"

"I told you. I tell her almost everything. *Almost.*"

168

Chapter 33: Skye

Priscilla is shooting me a horrified look. I can't blame her. My disfigured face belongs to someone who needs to go to the emergency room right away.

She drives me in her Prius. I called her out of the blue, asking her to pick me up at the edge of the park. When Priscilla saw me, she was appalled. She wanted to call 911 and asked me a barrage of questions, but I told her I needed time. I was adamant about not going to a hospital or involving the cops.

Protecting the Veil means I don't get much medical attention or police help.

I couldn't call Yara or Greta. They would be curious about me, the Singularity, and the Night covens. It would be just a matter of time before they realized that, if the Night covens have questions about Brianna, our covens should look into that too.

That's not the main reason, though. I'm not sure I trust them. They drugged me without my knowledge. It's a shame, because Yara probably knows how to brew a mean Healing potion.

They are my Sisters, but I feel more connected to Pri.

I can't show up like this at Gemma's house. She'd immediately call Mum—or worse, Connor. The last thing I need is Connor getting even more suspicious. He's already pushing me to meet that Mother with Truth Charm, and I have no idea how to get out of it.

Priscilla steals some glances my way. Knowing her, I'm sure she will press me for answers soon.

I flip down the passenger's mirror. Oh, Goddess. My real face has disappeared. I'm looking at a grotesque mask made of dirt, blood, and dead skin. My old arm and temple scars from the battles with Jane were finally gone, but now this: my face is swollen, covered in bruises, and my nose may be broken. Great.

Please, let the Allure work its magic. No way can I be seen in public like this. I need to accelerate my healing.

The pain is crazy. I've never experienced anything like this. It feels like an insanely bad sinusitis, only it acts on my whole face. Thank Goddess Priscilla brought me the bag of ice I asked for. I press it to my face with care, and it soothes me a little.

"Can I have a sleep over?" I mumble with a hoarse voice.

"Sure," Priscilla says. "Skye—"

"Please, listen to me. Can you take me to my house first? I need to get some stuff, and then we can go to yours. We'll talk later."

"That's not cool, Skye."

"Just give me a few minutes for myself. Please?"

She shakes her head and says, "Fine."

Minutes later, we're in front of Gemma's house. She's used to my coming home late, and all the lights are out. Still a bit dizzy, I walk to the front door, unlock it, and punch in the security code.

The dark house is silent. If Gemma catches me and sees my face, I'm done for. She'll call all the Sisters she knows, starting with Mum and Connor. I tiptoe to my room and gather my ritual tools and some vials that Yara prepared. I stuff a few clothes into a duffel bag.

I scribble a note for Gemma. "Sleeping over at Priscilla's. I will call you when I wake up." It sounds detached. So I add, "Love, Skye." I slide the note under her door.

When I get back to the car, Priscilla is tapping her fingers on the steering wheel. She's about to burst.

"Thanks, Pri. You're always there for me."

This softens her a little. She raises her eyebrows, but drives me to her home in silence.

Her house is as dead as mine. We go to her room.

"I need a few minutes in your bathroom," I tell her.

She nods. "Do you need help?"

"Maybe later. Thanks." I take all my stuff into the bathroom.

With the lights on, I look at myself in the mirror. Rather, I look at the house of horrors version of myself who is staring back at me. I need to see what's underneath the red mask. I wash my hands thoroughly. Cold water splashed on my face soothes the pain a little. It washes the blood away. I repeat the process until the water runs almost clear. I get a hand towel and gently pat my face with it. The towel turns pink.

Now I can see all the damage. My nose is huge and looks crooked, but it doesn't feel broken. At least, it doesn't hurt worse than the rest of my face. Maybe it's just swollen.

My lips and brow are covered with cuts. Both my cheeks are puffed up. I've got a black eye and a chipped tooth. It's surreal, like I've fought an MMA match.

I rummage in my duffel bag and line up Yara's vials. It's too late for the Shield pill now—and even the Shield ritual I did this morning was cancelled by the Dispel tattoo. The Shield spell could have lessened the effects of the beating too, but it's much better to have had the Dispel and not spilled the beans about Mona.

I should have made an amulet for me, just like I did for Mona.

The Shield pills and the attack ones—Sleep, Poison Ivy, Decay—go back into the duffel bag.

If the Dispel works like the other potions, it should have worn off by now. I fill a glass of water and take Restore and Healing pills. Yara, despite my mixed feelings about you, I can't deny you're a master of potions.

I find a bottle of Advil behind the vanity mirror and take the full daily dose. Pri knocks quietly on the door.

"Hey, there you are. You look much better," she says after I let her in.

"Thanks for lying, Pri."

"You're welcome. Here, I found Neosporin. I can make a pharmacy run if you need."

"No, thanks. That will do. Apply it for me?"

"Sure. Sit on the edge of the bathtub and close your eyes."

She's in better spirits. Or at least, she's faking it. Either way, I'm glad. I feel bad about lying to her.

The cold cream against my face is soothing. I hope all the drugs kick in soon.

"So crazy night, huh?" she says.

"Pri, I'm sorry, but I can't tell you everything." Thank Goddess my eyes are closed. I don't want to see her disapproving face.

"You know that's not normal, right? I mean, a few weeks ago I saw scars on your head and arms. And now this. What's going on?"

"I can't tell you. I really can't."

"It's not Drake, right?"

"No!"

"Or your creepy ex?"

172

"No! He's not creepy, just…an idiot."

I hear a sigh. "Then it's worse. If it's not them, a stranger did this to you. You need to tell the police. Or social services. You're still a minor. And you need, I don't know, a bodyguard. Open your eyes, Skye."

I open them and stare at her. But I understand she means that I need to see the situation.

Her face looks older, stern. "Skye. What's going on? Tell me. Don't you trust me?"

My eyes water. "Pri, I trust you more than anyone. You're the best. I just can't tell you everything."

Priscilla's tone is a disheartened one. "You rescued me when I hit rock bottom with Boulder's accident. Think about it. Imagine how helpless I feel when I see him like that and now you like this, and you won't let me do anything for you. Let me help you."

I put my hand over hers. "You can't. No one can. But it's okay. It's over. Don't worry. Promise me you won't worry."

She's not sold. "Promise me you will tell me and ask me for help if it gets worse."

"Deal."

We go to sleep in her queen-sized bed. She strokes my hair until I black out.

***

Bright lights. This is wrong. Am I in London? No, no, I'm in Seattle. Either way, this is wrong.

My head hurts. It feels heavy. Even my eyelids are made of lead. Opening my eyes is a tricky proposition.

I blink a few times. The bed feels odd—too soft. The walls are different. Priscilla's bedroom.

Memories from the previous night hit me like a tsunami. I'm awash in pain, tension, and confusion. Miranda and Jane in one night. Being drugged by my own friends, and then beaten up by my enemies. That was a serious beating.

Breathing deeply, I calm my nerves. I'm safe now. In Pri's house. Her bedroom is my little sanctuary. I'm so glad I have a friend.

Then I turn and see Priscilla's face, and I'm not so glad anymore.

She's staring at me with an accusatory gaze: narrowed eyes, a deep scowl, her lips glued together. What did I do this time? I mean, besides keeping my best friend in the dark?

"How do you feel?" Her words are affable, but her tone sure isn't.

"Better." My voice comes out in a growl, so I clear my throat and try again. "Not well, but better. It couldn't get worse, could it?" I say, offering an ice-breaker.

But somehow her expression becomes even sterner. "I'd say it could," she says. She shows me a bag full of pills and vials. Yara's stash.

My mind is dull and slow. I can't understand exactly what's going on. I come back with the lamest of the responses: "Did you go through my things?"

"That's not the issue here, Skye."

I try to prop myself up on the fluffy pillows, but I drown in them. "It sounds like a pretty important issue. To me."

"Don't be so righteous. You brought drugs into my house. But that's also *not* the issue."

With considerable effort, I straighten, despite the quicksand-ish pillows. I lean against the back board of the bed, but lifting my head makes me dizzy.

"Pri, I'm confused… These are not drugs."

She throws the bag on my lap. "I'm not an idiot! This bag and last night proves you're involved in drugs. And drug deals. That's what you were doing there, right? A deal gone bad?"

I snort, but the sudden movement feels like my brain is about to explode. My nose hurts like hell too. I groan and bring my hands to my face, but manage to whisper, "You've been watching too much cable, Pri."

"What is it, then? What happened last night?" She slaps the bed.

"Can you get me a glass of water?"

"No. Tell me. Right now, straight up, before you have time to think up a lie. The scars, the beating, the drugs."

"Those are not drugs. Those are supplements."

"What?"

"Organic stuff. Mortar and pestle, my little cauldron, some herbs." I open the bag. "Come on, smell it." I hand her over a sage leaf. "It's natural."

"Like weed?" She picks up the leaf and takes a whiff.

"No. Like a natural medicine. That's why I had to get it last night. I believe in this. I haven't looked in the mirror, but I bet I'm already looking better. Or, at least, not too messed up. Right?"

She eyes me strangely, but nods in an almost imperceptible motion. Goddess bless the Allure and Yara's bag of tricks.

"It works. You can buy these in shops—it's nothing illegal. And I don't get high or anything."

"You are a new age kook…" Pri says, unsure.

"Thanks."

"But you put on Neosporin. And I saw the Advil bottle."

I shrug pointedly. "Just hedging my bets."

"What about this?" She points to my face.

"It was a mugging, Pri. Did you see my wallet or my cell? He took them. I was just too pissed off to talk about it last night. Even my glasses are gone," I add, for effect.

"You called me on a phone." She fishes the phone Jane gave me out of my purse.

It takes me few seconds, but I come up with an explanation. "This is a prepaid, cheap one that I keep for when the battery of the other is dead. Or for emergencies. Like this." What's another lie?

Her lips are still pursed. But her voice is low now. "Were you attacked…you know?"

"No, no. That would be horrific. No, just some thug trying to get my purse, and me dumbly fighting him off. Don't worry."

I tell her I was in the park for one of my "silly nature walks," and a guy came and tried to rob me. When I resisted, he beat me to take my purse—and punched me a little extra, for my daring.

"Oh, Skye, that sounds terrifying."

"It was."

She looks at me with pity now. "And your scars?"

I point to my temple. "This one I got at the pool, watching Drake. I slipped and hit my head. He was there; you can ask him. And this one," I show her the almost invisible scar on my arm, "I got it when I was using that knife in the bag." I point to my athame. "I was trying to chop some leaves. You know how clumsy I am."

She nods, deep in thought. "Why didn't you tell me any of these things?"

I open my arms. "I don't know. Those are all embarrassing. All that happened because I like alternative stuff. And you're not into any of that. I was afraid you would think I was a dork."

"That's dumb. I already think that." Her mouth almost smiles.

"Now, can we get into why you were going through my stuff?"

"Just concerned with my sis." Pri taps my knee affectionately. "You told you would call Gemma in the morning. Here's the phone. Do you want the glass of water now?"

"If the interrogation is over," I say.

***

During breakfast, I tell Priscilla, "I need to call Drake. I don't want him to see me like this."

Priscilla stops making pancakes and looks at me with raised eyebrows. "Ooh, intrigue and deception."

"I don't like to lie to him, but if he sees this," I say, pointing to my face, "he'll freak out."

"It would be a warranted freak out, just so you know. Okay, we need a good excuse. Figure it out and blame me. Everybody does," she says, while depositing one more flapjack into my plate.

"I could tell him we're going away on a girl's road trip. What do you think?"

Pri bites her lip. "Sorry. I've been to the hospital almost every day since the accident. If I went away and something happened…" Her voice trails off.

"We don't need to actually go anywhere."

"Ooh, Skye, you wicked girl. But what if I bump into Drake at the hospital?"

"Let's just figure it out as it goes."

She throws me her cell and sits down to gorge on the pancakes. It's weird seeing this paper-thin girl stuff herself with carbs.

"Hey, my man," I tell Drake when he picks up.

"Miss Lexington-Ellis, how are you this morning? Too cool for school today?"

"Yeah, I decided to take a day off." Oops, I need to call the school.

"I wish you had told me. We could hang out together. Wait, are you calling from Priscilla's phone?"

"Yeah, I lost mine."

"You can say that again," Priscilla mumbles with her mouth full.

"Seriously, again?" Drake asks. "You need to wear them on a necklace." Then his voice gets serious. "Listen, can you meet me—"

"No, that's what I wanted to tell you. Pri and I are going on a road trip this weekend."

"But it's Thursday," he points out.

"Yes, it's just that we need some girl time."

"Okay…" He sounds disappointed. Sorry, Drake.

"What did you want to tell me?"

"No, nothing. We'll talk when you get back. What about school? Where are you going?"

Priscilla takes the phone away from me. "Don't know yet. Probably Mount Si. Snowboarding, maybe. Now, if you will excuse us, we need to go shopping for the trip. Take care." She hangs up.

"Pri!"

"What? That would've taken hours." She sits down again and takes another bite of her pancake. "He would have asked too many questions."

"What now?"

"Let's just stay in and watch a ton of movies."

Chapter 34: Drake

Skye said she would return soon. It's been five days now. I don't know what to expect. She's missing school and doesn't care. Is she going on secret missions now? Is she a witch spy?

It occurs to me that a globe-trotting secret agent was the wish-fulfillment illusion I once created to justify my mother's absence. How ironic if my girlfriend ended up being exactly that and abandoning me—even if it's just for a few days.

It's just five p.m., but nightfall has arrived. I hate this part of the year. So dark and gloomy.

I'm alone. With Dad still at work and Mona spending the night at Pain's, the house is all mine. Again. Sean is at the hospital with Boulder, but later he'll go home to work on his writing. No other names to call pop into my head. A reminder that I don't have many friends.

Huh. Is that what being lonely means? I didn't feel like that before meeting Skye.

I have no idea why her sudden trip makes me so uneasy. The thought of her not coming back has crossed my mind. But I respect her. I trust her. I never will be the obsessive, controlling boyfriend. She will tell me when she does.

Someone is knocking at the front door. We should put up a sign.

I have no patience for solicitors. Because I always, *always* cave in.

I open the door and pull back out of instinct.

Jane is here.

But she's not the Jane I remember. In front of me, I see a pale, tame version of her, with half her face covered in thin scars, the other half deformed in a gruesome burn, and blood soaking the side of her jacket.

"Help me," she croaks. "Please."

I want to punch her. I have all the reasons in the world to slam the door in her face. I should call 911.

But what dumb me does, of course, is catch her when her legs give out.

Damn it, damn it, damn it!

My eyes still scan her hands for signs of weapons or potions. She is still Jane, after all.

"Lean on me," I say.

She lets part of her weight rest on my arms. With my support, she stumbles into my living room. I lead her to the sofa and deposit her there carefully.

Jane grunts and sits sideways, looking at me with a blank stare. Her forehead is covered in sweat; her lips are almost white.

I rush to the linen closet in search of towels. While I get them from the shelves, I can almost hear part of my brain screaming to get away from her, to tie her up, to throw her out. However, the other side of my brain—the boy scout side—is unflappable.

When I get back, Jane is still in the same position. I motion for her to lift her hand from the wound. I remove her jacket with care. She raises her shirt slowly, and I see a gash with blood seeping out.

"Put this over it and keep pressure on it," I say, handing her a towel. "Were you shot?"

Her answer is almost inaudible. "Stabbed."

I reach for my cell.

"Don't," her wisp of a voice tells me.

"I need to call an ambulance. I know the cops are after you, but you may die."

Jane shakes her head slowly. The vulnerability in her gesture is so evident, I don't dial.

"I need Skye," she says. "I…" She takes a deep breath, and then she lets out a rush of words, "I won't bleed to death, but the wound is poisoned. I need a potion. Only a potion."

The effort of saying so much takes a toll on her, and Jane gasps for air, her eyes desperate and vulnerable. *Jane.*

"Skye is away, Jane."

She stares at me with a guilty look at her face. Then she casts her eyes down.

"Mona?" she whispers without looking at me.

Something inside me snaps. "That's it, isn't it? A trap? You know Skye is not here, so you show up wounded to get some pity out of me and make me hand you Mona on a plate? Is that blood even real? I hope you didn't mutilate yourself just to get to my sister. That's low even for you, Jane."

I motion to get my cell from my pocket. She slowly raises her hand to stop me, but she misses me completely. I expect her to turn and hit me, but she just stays there, one hand compressing the wound, the other waiving aimlessly, completely defeated.

Not even her helplessness will stop me from calling the cops now.

But then she opens her damn mouth again and pleads, "Don't. They will kill him."

"Him?"

It's like time is standing still. Jane is bleeding on my sofa, and I'm torn between calling 911 and handing her over to the police and hearing more of her B.S.

"Who's 'him', Jane? What game are you playing now?"

She grunts. "I don't need Mona or Skye. Just find any witch who can make me a potion. Do you know any others?"

Is that a gambit? Anyway, I do know the Weird Sisters.

My mind races faster than I can follow it. If I bring Greta or Yara here, they'll know about Jane. And Jane knows about Mona's secret. I can't risk that. But I must help Jane.

"Hold on. What kind of potion?"

"Do you know a witch? Let me talk to her."

"No, I have potions upstairs. Skye left some."

Yes, she did. To protect Mona and me from, of all the people on the planet, Jane. How's that for ironic?

"What do you have?" she croaks.

I know it's a risk telling Jane all the defenses we have against her, but we're past that point now.

"A few Shield, one Energy, one Blinding, four Sleep, a Dispel—"

"You have a Dispel?" For the first time, Jane is alert.

"Yeah. Let me finish: a Night Sight, a Clean Plate—"

"Do you mean a Clean Slate?"

"I guess."

Jane's free hand points at me weakly. "That's the one."

"Are you sure? Skye said it was for magical diseases."

"It'll work on this poison."

I rush upstairs, fetch the vial, and climb down the steps two-by-two. I'm relieved that Mona is not coming home tonight. It'd be hard

182

to explain what Jane is doing in our living room before my sister exploded or something.

When I get back, Jane is still in the same place.

"Do you drink or pour it over the wound?" I ask.

Jane looks at me. "Maybe pour?" That's what she does.

The liquid coming in contact with the wound produces a white foam and a crackling noise.

She grits her teeth.

I hand her a clean towel. "We still need an antiseptic."

"No, the potion will take care of infections. I just need to stop the bleeding."

The gash is not too deep. I clean her wound and bandage it. "Keep an eye on it. It might not hold."

"I need water." Her voice is still weak, but clearly better than before.

I bring a pitcher and two glasses. We look at each other while drinking.

"Thanks," she says, adding to the surrealism of the night.

"Why didn't you call Connor? You were lovers and all."

"Connor is not like you. He wouldn't trust me. He'd hand me over, or leave me to die."

"You don't know me at all. Now that you're not going to die, I'll call the police."

Jane shakes her head again, but now she is the one looking at me with pity. "No, you won't," she says softly. "If you wanted to do it, you would already have done it. And I know why you don't want to do it. You think I'll expose Mona. Or break the Veil."

"Wouldn't you?"

"I'm here precisely to prevent that. Mona's secret is what's

183

keeping my brother alive."

"What?"

"Just give me a minute."

***

We've changed Jane's bandage once already, hoping the new one will hold better. Jane finished eating a few crackers and took the Stamina and Restore potions I found. Now she's drinking juice from a bottle. We're still in my living room, like normal people. Like she's visiting.

Please, please don't let me regret this.

"Jane, I'll hear your story, but you must know this: I'll never let you hurt Mona or Skye again. I might not be a witch, but I can get rid of you."

She tries to smile, but the corners of her mouth point down. "You'll never kill me, Drake. It's not in you."

"I can do other things. Put you in jail and run away with Mona. Ask her to brew a Forget potion so strong, you'll have permanent amnesia."

Jane's eyebrows go up. "You're right. She would have personal magic enough to pull that off. Is she brewing potions already?"

"Jane!"

She lifts a hand up. "Force of habit. It won't happen again."

"Just tell me what's up with your brother."

She drinks the last of the juice and stares at the empty bottle. "I know you might not believe it, but I'm sorry for what I did to your sister and your girlfriend."

"Right…"

"I am sorry! Well, not sorry for them, to tell the truth. Sorry for my choices."

184

"You're unbelievable. That's not an apology at all!"

"It's the best I can offer. Hear me out. What I mean is, I didn't want to kill anyone. I had to."

I snort. "Nobody 'has to' kill, Jane."

"Really? What if they got Mona and told you that you had to kill to keep her alive?"

I ponder that. "There would be other ways…"

"Not for some people, there wouldn't! That's what the Night covens did to my brother. I had to find the Singularity and steal her power, or they'd murder him."

***

I can't believe I'm entertaining Jane. Dad has just called saying he'll work late again. I had forgotten about him. Those bloodstains on the sofa will be hard to explain. Since we have time, I'll try to extract as much information from Jane as I can.

The effort of maintaining a calm conversation with her is physically taxing; my back stiffens, my muscles ache, my head feels heavy. I draw short breaths.

"If you want me to listen to you, you should tell me the whole story. I mean everything."

We're both surprised at my harsh tone. What can I say? I want to get to the bottom of this, and it's time to stop playing around.

Jane's bleeding has stopped, and the color is returning to her damaged cheeks. "Fair enough," she says.

Somehow, "fair" and "Jane" don't seem to belong in the same universe.

"When the Night covens found me—"

"Wait, Jane. The whole story. Come on, it's your show. I want your full bio."

"You wish." Her face darkens. That's the Jane I remember.

"No deal, then. Let's go back to hoping our siblings will survive."

"Fine. You want to know? We're from Idaho. When my parents found out I was a Sister, they kicked me out. I was fifteen."

"That's harsh."

"To be honest, it was a relief. Living with them wasn't…safe. That's why I took Jason with me."

"Your brother?"

"Yes. I was fifteen, and he was ten. Ten! We ran away to Spokane. A Mormon family, the Neills, took us in. My original family never went looking for us; the Neills never questioned us after we told them the situation we had come from. I don't even know if, legally, we could have stayed with them. They told family and friends that we were orphans, and that was the end of it. The Neills were great to us. Of course, they didn't know about the Craft."

It's hard to imagine ruthless Jane with a loving family. Well, after her not-so-loving real family rejected her.

She leans over. "That's when I met Cillian. He was a boy from Spokane, a male witch. I was working at a Burger King, and we sensed each other when he drove through one day. You know about witch sense, right?"

I nod.

"He drove past the drive-through window, parked, and came to talk to me. He told me I was wasting my talent, and that he could teach me magic."

"And you went with him."

"You don't understand. Imagine if Mona—I'm not asking about her, by the way—imagine if she didn't have Skye to guide her. How lost would she be? What if she didn't have a family or a future and a charming guy with this kick-ass gift entered her life, saying she could do whatever she wanted, be whoever she wanted? *Of course*, I went with him."

"And Jason?"

"He had the Neills. He was better off without me." She checks the bandage. "I just hopped into Cillian's car and rode to Seattle with him. He taught me the basics, took me to get the silver tat. I was seventeen then. Yes, we lived together. What's this stare? You're judging me, aren't you?"

"I didn't say anything."

"Right," she says, not convinced. "But I didn't fall for him. I liked him, and I idolized him. He was my everything, but I didn't love him. He had a Seduction Charm. That's why I ran away with him; that's why I stayed with him. And he taught me magic. Only, it was Night magic."

"Didn't it upset you?"

"It did. At the time, I didn't know it was Night magic: for all I knew, it was the *only* magic in existence. I thought I was a witch, and that was magic, and that was that. I didn't even meet his coven." She shrugs. "Then things took a turn for the worse. He was drinking. Taking potions to get high. He beat me up. Forced me to do…things. That wasn't any better than what I had left in Idaho." She raises her eyes and mutters, "Crap."

If that's true, I feel for her. *If* it's true.

Neither of us knows how or wants to discuss the elephant in the conversation, so she just goes on.

"The beatings got worse. Sometimes it got real bad, but he'd fix me with potions and spells. He never let me go to a hospital. This nose," she points to her face, "wasn't like that. So once again, I ran away. I knew some things and had hidden some money from him. I just lay low. I knew how to avoid Cillian. I used the only magic I knew, Night magic, to survive. Sold drugs, slipped Sleep potions into guys' drinks so I could get their money. It was a living. But one day, Mona's energy wave hit all of us."

"The thing that alerted the covens?"

"Yes, that 'thing.' The Singularity had arrived. I had no idea what it meant at the time. Then Cillian found me."

"How?"

"If you know how to brew a Truth potion, and you're a willing Night witch, you can be quite persuasive. He knew about my Charms. I had stolen his energy accidentally a few times, so he knew about my Magical Absorption."

"You mean, your Steal Charm."

She scowls. "Okay. My *Steal* Charm. It was the cause of a few beatings, actually. He was paranoid and thought I was doing it on purpose." Then her eyes glaze over, and she stops talking altogether.

I give her a minute. Oh, boy, what did they do to Jane? Nobody should go through that. Her scarred face makes me empathize with her even more. "Do you need anything? Water? Aspirin?"

"No," she says with pride. "He introduced me to Miranda, who told me all about the Singularity and the Search. She is one of the lieutenants in charge of the Search. That's when I first learned about regular magic—the kind Skye and most covens practice. Miranda told me she wanted to make sure her coven was the one to find the Singularity. And that, in case they found her, they would ensure they'd have the Singularity's power."

"They wanted you to steal her magic."

"I said yes just to get out of there. But then Cillian took me home, and everything started again. The covens found me and took Jason as insurance. After Cillian died."

"He died?"

"It was an accident. Sort of. It was self-defense," Jane says with no emotion.

I stare at her, stunned. Jane is indeed a killer. No doubt she had the potential; I mean, I saw her trying to kill Skye. But to know, to hear it from her lips, it's chilling.

"You don't know what it was like." She's not defiant anymore. "But he had already told Miranda about Jason, and she took him. They made me do it. You think I'm bad. I'm not. I did what I had to do to get my brother back. *They* are the bad guys."

If any other person had told me this story, I'd probably side with her right away. But this is Jane, so I weigh everything. This could be all part of a trap, or a delusion. And we have baggage. She's the enemy. She made herself my enemy.

But I believe her. She's had many chances to get Mona already. If this is her real story, I can't help but understand where she is coming from.

"Which leads me to tonight and this," she points to her wound. "I saw when they took Skye—"

"They took Skye?"

"Not tonight, dummy. Last time."

"What time?"

She blinks a few times.

"Jane!"

"She didn't tell you? Miranda kidnapped Skye and almost killed her. You saw her face, didn't you?"

I want to grab Jane and shake her. "What are you talking about?

Do they have Skye now?"

"No, they left her for dead. Last Wednesday. Almost a week ago. She was okay. Beaten up, but okay."

All the puzzle pieces that were putting themselves together after Jane's story now scramble in different directions. Skye was almost killed. Again!

And she didn't tell me. Why?

A sudden headache hits me. My cheeks are cold. I hate that I don't know what's going on. My hands press my temples as if to squeeze out the pain inside.

"Wow," Jane says. "I thought she told you everything."

"Don't twist the knife, Jane." My voice is a snarl. "Wait. How do you know that? And what's up with her face?"

"I was watching Miranda and her coven. From a distance, so they wouldn't sense me. I hoped it would lead me to Jason. That's when I saw Skye. She spent about three hours in there. I followed them when they left—again, I thought they might take her to the same place they're hiding my brother. But they just left her at the park. Her face was destroyed."

"Jane, you—"

"Calm down. The Allure will fix her. And I made sure she was alive."

I'm still confused, but this last bit of information jumps out. "*You* made sure she was alive?"

Despite her wound, Jane is perched at the edge of the seat. "Of course. I need her."

"You need her for what?"

"To find Jason! He is surrounded by Sisters. Skye has the witch radar, right?"

"How do you know?"

"Cillian's Charms. Seduction and Intuition. I got them. Seduction is how I got you and Connor to…cooperate. That and the Fancy Me potions—you had no chance. And when Skye sensed me from far away at the park, something clicked in my head. My Intuition helped me figure out what it was. The Intuition also told me to follow Mona on the day of the earthquake."

Jane is becoming this super-witch—how many Charms does she have now? Four? I shudder, thinking of her with all this power. But I have other priorities now.

This strange night is getting stranger by leaps and bounds.

"Why did they kidnap Skye?"

"I'm guessing they did it to know about the Singularity, since they think your girlfriend is the one who collected the prize."

"Do they know about Mona?"

"I'd bet that they know now."

"Skye would never talk."

She slaps her hand on her leg. "You still don't get it, right? It doesn't matter how tough she is. They have Truth potions."

No, no!

Jane says, "But, Mona is still safe, right? If Skye had talked, they'd have taken Mona by now. Why would they wait?"

"Maybe they have a plan? Maybe they don't want to attract attention?"

Jane loses her cool. "I don't know what you're thinking. Because those guys don't give a damn about the Veil. The Night covens are much more powerful. They run the world. They steamroll everything. Once they get their hands on your precious sister, they will use her power—*very* publicly. And if they can't, they will kill her. If they can't have her, they'll make sure no one else will." She pants. "I was their golden ticket. Do you know how rare the…Steal Charm is? I'm the only one they know with it. Maybe I'm the only one who has it! But they wanted me to be their slave, not their queen."

I can barely breathe. I try to enunciate my words. "What does it matter? You're still *you*. Why are you telling me this?"

She hesitates. She lowers her eyes and looks at her fingers. "I told you. I need Skye to find Jason." Her voice becomes icy. "And if I can't, I want revenge. I can't kill them. But I can stop them from getting what they want the most."

Wow, maybe she is insane. "I'll never let you near my sister. Ever. Again."

She nods as I speak. "Of course not. That's not what I am asking."

"What, then?"

"I want you to help me kill Brianna." She looks at me as if *she* is exasperated. "Isn't it obvious?"

I stare at her for a few seconds. Maybe it's a joke—a bad joke. Maybe she's just trying to confuse me. If that's her intention, she's succeeding. I think hard but come up empty. "No. It's not obvious at all."

She sighs. "If Brianna dies, everybody will think the Singularity is dead. They may let Jason walk. They'd have no reason to keep him. The Night covens will never have a reason to go after Mona." Her eyes have a glint. A sense of triumph. "Drake, no one will ever know about Mona."

Even my slow brain catches up. "Not even the other covens," I mumble, mostly to myself.

Jane nods again. The glint is still there.

"You will know," I say. "You want Mona's power. You just don't want to share it with the other psychos."

"Is this how you believe me?"

"Okay, I need to ask. I thought you wanted Mona to find Jason. Why didn't you just steal her powers?"

"So your opinion of me hasn't really changed, has it? Are you asking why I didn't kill your sister?"

"Let's just say the old Jane—"

"I'm the same Jane. I won't kill someone if I don't have to do it."

I point my finger at her. "Jane, that's not the point. I'm sorry for what happened to you and Jason, but it doesn't justify... It *never* justifies killing someone."

"Don't be so righteous. And give me some credit. Even I know that I'm playing with destiny if I kill someone's sister to save my own brother."

"You understand how this is hard for me to believe, don't you?"

She looks away. "I promise you I won't go after Mona. I promise. I'm here, and we didn't try to kill each other. That's progress, right?"

"Jane, do you realize that what you're asking—"

She stares at me. "Listen to me. I won't touch Mona. It'd be like killing a unicorn." She sees my fake-shocked look and answers my mental question. "No, unicorns don't exist. It's a figure of speech, stupid."

"Why would I trust you? I want to believe you. I really do, Jane, but give me a reason."

She scoffs. "Nobody trusts me anymore, Drake. No one. You can be suspicious and do just what you think is safe. But I swear to you: my brother is in danger. I just hope he's still alive. Wouldn't you do anything for Mona? It's the same with me and Jason."

Chapter 35: Skye

Priscilla and I are watching one of the classics, "When Harry Met Sally", and gorging on gourmet popcorn when the doorbell rings.

"Pause, pause," she says. "I need to get the door." She stands up, knocking the bowl over.

"I'll clean it up," I offer. I get down on my knees and collect the popcorn off the floor, from between the cushions, and from under the sofa.

I'm so distracted that I don't see who comes in.

"Hey," Drake says.

I freeze, still kneeling, a handful of popcorn in my hand and probably a shocked expression on my face.

Behind Drake, a distressed Priscilla mouths, "I'm sorry."

He says to me, "Not looking good. What happened?"

My free hand touches my face where the swelling is at its worst. I finally come back to Earth and stand up. I turn to Priscilla, "Would you mind—"

"Not at all. I'll be in my room," she says. She climbs the steps in a hurry.

I sit down on the sofa, knocking the bowl over again, but this time I don't bother. Drake sits by my side.

"Are you okay?" His voice has no warmth.

"Yes. It's not as bad as it seems."

"It looks pretty bad to me."

"How did you know?" I ask.

"We'll talk about that later. First, tell me what happened."

I'm ashamed. I look around as if asking for support, but the only friendly face in the room is Meg Ryan's on the screen. Worst of all, Drake seems angry. He hasn't even touched me.

There's no point in lying now. I tell him everything.

When I'm done, he stays silent. Then he snorts, but not in an amused way. "We keep having the strangest conversations, don't we?"

I don't answer.

He looks at me. "So to recap: you were drugged by the Weird Sisters—supposedly, your friends. You trusted a guy you had met only once before to give you a ride and ended up kidnapped. Then you refused Jane's help. Finally, you didn't tell me any of it. And you lied to me. Again."

"You're twisting it a little bit," I point out.

"Don't you think you have a problem? Why do you always trust the wrong people?"

I don't like being accused. "Am I supposed to trust Jane now?"

"For what it's worth, this time she tried to help you. And she's the one who told me what happened to you."

"What?"

"She showed up at my house last night, bleeding badly. We stopped the blood loss with potions and stuff, and then she told me the weirdest story. She has a brother, Jason, who's a prisoner of the Night covens. They were blackmailing her into finding the Singularity and stealing her power."

"And you believed Jane?"

"There's no excuse for what she did, but it's a good explanation."

"The woman who beat me up, Miranda, mentioned something about Jason. She wanted to kill him. But don't you see? Miranda and Jane might have created this story to fool us."

Drake stands up. "No, they didn't. Why would they do that? They could just get Mona and be done with it."

I look down, inadvertently staring at the fancy, fluffy white carpet. Priscilla's house, so accommodating a few minutes ago, doesn't look that cozy anymore. I'm getting tired of being the bad guy in this conversation. "You talk about trust. What are you doing entertaining Jane? Why do you trust her now?"

"Why? To be honest, I had every motive to throw her out. But I believe her story."

"You're too trusting, Drake. It's just who you are. Remember when you gave your coffee money to the homeless man? I saw that. That's the same thing. *Too* trusting. Couldn't it be a scam?"

"That's possible. But then I think: if it is, I'm just losing five or ten bucks to a con. But what if it isn't? I may be helping him to get one more meal, one more warm night. It could make a difference. It's a bet, and I prefer to bet on the good side."

"Even with Jane?"

He paces the room. "Especially with Jane. If there's a chance we can turn her around, it's our responsibility to try."

"Even with Mona's life at stake? If you're wrong, it's not ten bucks you're going to be losing."

His confidence is shaken, but he recovers soon. "But what if she is telling the truth and holds up her side of the bargain? Mona would be safe."

"Oh, Drake…"

"Terrible things happened to Jane when she was a kid. She was acting desperate."

"I'm sorry for her, but so what? Terrible things happened to you, and you don't try to kill people."

"It's different. And she doesn't have a friend, not even someone to use as a sounding board. Come on, Skye. I believe she's being honest, but we can still be careful. Have a failsafe. We can help her."

"That's the smart move too."

"What do you mean?"

I hate the practical, calculating thought I'm about to voice, but he needs to be aware of it. "Imagine she's telling the truth and that she loses her brother because we didn't help. She'll blame us. Can you imagine Jane's wrath then? Even if she couldn't hurt Mona, she'd expose the Singularity for sure."

"In Jane's defense, she has never threatened to do that."

"She doesn't need to, Drake. We know what's she's capable of, right?"

"I like to have faith in people," he says.

I lose my patience. "Drake, I have no idea what's going on with you lately."

"Me neither. All we've been through, and you still don't trust me!"

"I didn't want to worry you."

"We're together! We're supposed to worry about each other. That's the whole point."

It's my turn to stand up and pace the room. I stop by the mantel, play with the Tiki trinkets on it. "What about these arguments? Are we supposed to be having them too?"

For the first time since he has arrived, he approaches me. "We're just having different opinions, Skye. Come on." He caresses my face. His touch is so soft; it doesn't hurt my swollen cheeks.

I lean my face against his hand, welcoming his gesture, but I'm not convinced. "Okay, sweet-talking guy. But you need to go. We're having a girl's day in. We'll talk later. I still cannot appear in public like this."

Drake kisses me, but this time, there's no spark. He leaves.

It's like I don't know him anymore.

Drake and I have been disagreeing a lot lately. We've been at odds not about little things, like places to eat or movies to watch, but about important matters: the Veil, his Sister's life, maybe even ours.

Shouldn't we be on the same page? Not about everything, but at least on those crucial issues? If we aren't, maybe we're not as close as I thought. Maybe we're too different.

Chapter 36: Drake

Another day, another visit to the hospital. The updates the doctors give us are all starting to sound the same: Boulder is stable, but still critical. Some days he's slightly better; some days he gets a bit worse. As long as he's not *much* worse, I'm glad. He just needs a chance.

Jeff sees me and comes in my direction. I'm tall, and he still towers over me. When Jeff puts his hand on my shoulder and asks me to have a private conversation, I'm intrigued.

We go to a corner of the ICU's waiting room. His wife, Diana, is nowhere to be seen. Odd, because she is always at the hospital. Always. I start to dread the chat.

"How are you, Drake?"

He keeps his hands on my shoulders, his arms outstretched. I'm not sure if I'm supporting him, or if he is steadying me. Probably both.

"I'm well. Any news on Boulder?"

Jeff looks at me with a pained face. "That's what I want to talk to you about."

"Please don't tell me he's getting worse."

"Drake, do you know what hospice care is?"

Is that it? That's not so bad. Why is Jeff so worried? "I've heard about it. Are you taking Boulder home? That's good news, right?"

He hesitates before answering. "It is. Usually. Drake, Boulder's situation is unchanged. He is not getting better. He...*will not* get better."

Jeff's eyes don't let mine look away. He waits for the message to sink in.

"No. You're mistaken. If he's unchanged—"

"No progress, Drake. No mental function. Even if his body recovers, he will be...gone." Jeff chokes up. "We talked about it a couple of times. He was concerned about football, concussions, and paralysis. He told us—Diana and I—that he'd like us to—"

I press my hand against my head, as if trying to expel the thoughts. "Why are you telling me this?"

"Drake, you deserve to know. Diana and I like you very much. You always were a good influence on Boulder."

"Don't do it. There's still time!"

"It pains me more than anyone else. He's my son. At the time, Diana and I thought he was being dramatic. We couldn't fathom that a healthy, strong boy would be in this situation. But now it's real." He looks away. "I'm not saying we're doing it. I just want you to be prepared for when the time comes."

I shake my head and push Jeff's hands off of my shoulders. I want to punch something or someone. At the same time, I don't want my words to hurt Jeff. His pain is immense; I can't add to it.

"So the hospice care?"

"The doctors have cleared him to be moved. We want him at home. We have the space, the resources. Nurse care every minute of the day, plus hospital equipment. But he'll be home."

"You're not..." I force myself to say it "You're not taking him so he could...die at home. Are you, Jeff?"

Jeff just stares at me. "We just want him at home, so if the worst happens, he'll be surrounded by family."

I feel like screaming. Instead, I say. "Please don't give up on him, Jeff. A miracle could happen. Please hang on."

He nods, but his eyes have no sign of hope.

Chapter 37: Skye

I'm at Drake's house. The living room feels formal, alien. This time, neither of us suggests going to his bedroom. What a change from a few weeks ago.

"I'm glad you are back to normal again," Drake says.

I touch my face involuntarily. No more swelling, no more cuts. Once again, my Allure Charm came through. That, and a bunch of Healing potions. Thank you, Goddess.

"It feels okay."

"Does it still hurt?"

"Not anymore."

He nods. "Let's get some air."

We walk by Greenwood's shops. A bakery. An art gallery. A tattoo studio. The gray clouds above us promise rain is on its way. People on the street look down and walk fast. By contrast, the cars on the road move at a lazy pace.

Drake is distracted, but after a while his expression goes dark.

I don't say anything. When an ambulance passes by, its sirens disturbing the peace around us, Drake wakes from his reverie.

He turns to me. "Skye, Boulder is not getting better." He looks devastated. His eyes are sunken; his voice is low.

"I know."

"I don't think the doctors can do much more for him."

My eyes water. "Oh, Drake. I'm so sorry."

He looks at me. "But…"

"Yes?"

"But maybe we can do something for him."

"What do you mean?"

"You saved me, Skye. Twice. You know how to heal people."

"Oh, Drake. I'd love to. But it's different. With you, I only stopped your bleeding. I still have no idea how hurt you were. I lucked out. It was an advanced spell for me, but not a powerful one. It could even have backfired."

"But you can try."

How do I explain it to him? "It's not like that. If the Sisters could heal at will, we would be all over hospitals and emergency rooms. I mean, that would be worth breaking the Veil for, I agree. But we can do only minor things. Stop bleedings, soothe a burn, that kind of stuff. Even the Sisters who choose to be doctors, even the ones with Healing Charm, they have limited powers. We don't have the energy to do much more."

Drake gives me an intense stare. "Mona has the energy."

It is as if the ground vanishes beneath my feet. "You can't be serious!"

"I am. It's a desperate situation, Skye."

"You would risk your sister's life for your friend's? How would that work, Drake?"

"Are you concerned about Mona or the covens?"

"How can you even ask that?"

"It's a valid question!"

I want to slap him. "Drake, I *betrayed* my coven so Mona could have a normal life. You're going to make what I did all in vain. *And ruin her life.*"

"If you want to look at it that way, I—"

"It's the only way to look at it!"

"Really? Because when I look at it in a few—no, many—years from now what I'll see is something different. I'll remember that I could've helped Boulder and I didn't! Five, ten, fifty years from now, what's going to stay with me is that I had a chance to save my friend."

"It's a long shot. You'd be risking a lot for an outside chance to save him."

He puts his hands over mine and says in a calmer tone, "Not if we use Mona's powers. With her energy and your knowledge, you can do it. At least, you'd have a better chance, right?"

"Drake, it's too risky! There's a difference between obsession and righteousness. You're so blinded by your loyalty to him that you will put Mona in danger."

"A while ago you said that the Singularity decision was not yours to make, or mine. You said it was Mona's."

"No, in this case, it isn't. I know what could happen. If we do this, there's no way of telling if Boulder will get better. The only sure thing is that Mona will be exposed! She cannot control her magic. Worse, it could even backfire."

"Backfire?"

"It may backfire and damage him or make it impossible for him to recover." I try to calm down a bit and use a soothing voice. "Of course we know what we're doing when we use the Craft, but there's always a chance it can go wrong. Even though it's second nature for us. And Mona is not trained at all; the risk is huge."

"You and Mona can do it. You did it to save me and Brianna. Mona controlled her powers then."

"It was a desperate situation, Drake. We had no choice. You and Brianna would have died. And Mona is not controlling her powers as well now."

He looks into my eyes. "Boulder needs our help."

"But Boulder is taken care of; everything modern medicine can do for him will be done."

"It's just not enough. We can help, Skye. It's our duty to help."

"I love that you think like this. But we also have the duty to protect Mona, don't we?"

He breaks eye contact with me and takes his hand off mine. "I can't believe you don't agree with me. You risked a lot to do the right thing."

"That's exactly why we need to protect Mona."

"I've got to go."

"Drake?"

"I'll talk to you later. You have your big interview with Connor tomorrow, right?"

"No, that's in three days."

"Still, you have to be sharp to lie convincingly." He leaves me without a goodbye kiss.

I want to go after him, but something glues me to the spot.

***

"I'm glad you came, Pain," I tell her. "Should I call you Pain?"

She doesn't smile. Somehow her green lipstick doesn't clash with the piercings on her lips, or the purple hair with the right side shaved. "My name is Rebecca, but only authority figures call me that. You know, parents and teachers." She rolls her eyes.

"Pain it is, then," I say.

A seedling of a smile sprouts. "Cool." A gust of wind blows her hair over her face, but she doesn't brush it away.

We're at the top of the bleachers of the Aqua Theater by Green Lake. It's yet another cloudy, chilly day, and our privacy is assured here. Only die-hard joggers venture onto the track behind the theater. A man kayaks alone in the lake.

"Do you understand why I called you here by yourself?" I ask.

"So you didn't want Mona to know?"

"Kinda. I wanted to give you the option of choosing what you'll tell Mona. You're a Knowing now, which is special in itself. But the Sister you're close with is the Singularity. So you have responsibilities now. You need to understand them."

Her eyes narrow.

The wind makes me shudder. Sometimes being a goth has its advantages: Pain wears a long black trench coat and black leather gloves. I envy her warm clothes.

"I know you're best friends," I say. You care for her, right?"

Her spine becomes straight. "Yeah."

It's hard to broach the subject. We're not close. First, I need to lay the groundwork. "None of us planned this. But now that you know she's a Sister, you can never—ever—tell anyone about it. You, like us, have to guard it with your life. I know you didn't ask for it, but that's how things work."

Despite my straightforward words, she relaxes and says, "I'm cool with that."

I smile. "Almost as important: she's your responsibility now." I pause to let that sink in. "It's not much different from what you already do as a friend: support and trust each other, be confidantes, stay together."

She nods. "Be there for her."

"Right! But you also need to protect her. You're equals, but I need you to be kind of a guardian to her. She's too important. You'll be like a bodyguard."

"What do you mean?"

"Sometimes you'll need to rescue her from herself. Mistakes that we usually let our friends do, bad decisions we see through but say nothing: you must act when these things happen."

She tilts her head off to one side. "She'll hate me if I do that."

"I don't think so. But even if she does, you must protect her. Do you promise?"

She stares at the lake. I've lost my glasses, but I don't need them to see that Pain's aura must be deep red. Her affection for Mona is undeniable. I hate to do it, but I'm going to have to address that.

"You're true friends, Pain. If something happens, you two will overcome it."

She doesn't look at me. "It's not that," she mumbles.

"You like her, don't you?"

"Of course I do." It's weird seeing this tall, fearsome girl so vulnerable.

"Do you love her?"

Her head snaps back to look at me. Her pale face becomes paler. "What?"

"If I'm mistaken, I apologize. But I know you're in love. Since you never mentioned it to Mona, I'm guessing she's the…object of your affection."

Pain plays with one of her lip piercings. She turns it like a spinning wheel. Her eyes drift to the lake again.

I say, "I'd never intrude like that into your private life, but it's the Singularity we're talking about. I need to know. And I need to know that it won't be a problem."

"What if it was?"

"Will it be?" The truth is that I'd have to do something to Pain. I don't want to even think about it, much less voice it.

"No. Never."

"Do you want to talk about it?"

She won't look at me. "Does Mona know?"

"I'm not sure. She may suspect…something."

Pain searches her trench coat's pockets and lights up a cigarette.

"Are you…out yet?"

Her eyes still are adrift. "It's not like that." She blows a big cloud of smoke. "I'm not sure. I don't think I like girls. I just love Mona. I just know. You know how it is." Her sweet voice is such a disconnect from her tough girl image.

Then I get an urge to understand, and something compels me to ask, "How do you know?"

"How?"

"Yes. This is for me. How do you know you love someone?"

"I'd die for her. I'd die without her."

My chest tightens. Her words stick with me.

We both stare at the lake, our eyes searching for something that might not be there.

"That's all I needed to hear," I say. "You'll do great."

Drake and I need to talk soon. But for now, I have to focus on tomorrow, and how to beat Connor's interrogation and the Truth potion.

Chapter 38: Drake

The doorbell rings. Yara is here. I hope I'm not making a mistake. Well, multiple mistakes.

When I open the door, the smiliest girl in Seattle greets me.

"Hi, handsome," she says.

"Hi, Yara. I'm glad you came."

She walks in and says, "Are you kidding? I can always make time for you. How are your classes at Ballard?"

"I only go there twice a week. They are a little ahead of me, but I'm catching up."

"You know I go there too for advanced chem, right? Maybe you could give me a ride sometime." Yara gets close to me. Like, a Priscilla-level of closeness. She's invading my personal space with the confidence and purpose of the 82nd Airborne. I lean back by instinct, but Yara leans forward in response. I've got my back to the wall, literally.

Yara is about to kiss me again, and I don't know exactly how to stop her. But I have to. I gently hold her shoulders.

"We can't do that. I'm sorry. I have a girlfriend. Your friend."

Her smile vanishes, but it isn't replaced by a sad or angry expression. She just looks at me. "She's not here, is she?"

Still holding her shoulders, I say, "It's just not right. Come on, you know that."

She casts down her eyes. "Sometimes it *feels* right, Drake. You can't fault a girl for trying."

"I…just don't have these feelings for you, Yara."

Her eyes lose a little of their light. "Eh, Drake, don't dump me."

"I'm not. I can't dump you, because we were never involved in the first place."

This makes her take a step back, and my hand loses contact with her.

"Yara, do you understand? In some other situation, I'd love to get close to you, but I have my girl. What about Skye?"

"*What* about her? She's my friend, but just because she saw you first, it doesn't mean I need to make way, you know? We're not five. It's not like I have to give up on my feelings because she called dibs on you."

"In this case—"

"No. I'm not giving up. Why should I always be the one who yields? This has happened my whole life. I've been too respectful, too shy, too mindful. I've been passed over too many times. When is it my turn? When?"

I'm disarmed by her candor. A wave of empathy washes over me. "I know exactly how you feel," I say. Of course I do. That's exactly how I felt just a few months ago.

Once again, her face doesn't betray any animosity. Only her fingers tap her thigh.

"Okay," she says. "I have a proposition. Let's not finish this discussion just yet. Instead, why don't I keep this…connection between us on this shelf, here." Her hand mimics holding a box, and then she puts the invisible box on a similarly invisible shelf. "If our situation changes, we can always go back and open the box, what do you say?"

I blink a couple of times. "Sure." What else can I say?

"But you have to promise one thing: please don't be so self-conscious around me. I may kind of flirt with you without even realizing sometimes, but it's just for fun. I can't turn it off, really, and you make me feel guilty every time you draw back."

If it gets me out of this weird situation, I'm okay with it. "Deal," I say.

She offers her hand. We shake hands, but she holds mine a bit longer. She stares into my eyes, but I just smile. I hope no impeding signs of panic come from my expression.

"Good boy. Come with me."

She turns and, still holding my hand, pulls me after her to the sofa. We sit down, and she finally lets go of my hand.

"See? I'm harmless." She grins.

"It's hard to think of you as harmless, Yara," I say. "Sorry."

"Sorry for what? This is one of the sweetest things someone has ever said to me." She points her finger at me. "You too flirt without even noticing, don't you?"

I shrug. "I wouldn't know. I really wouldn't."

"So what did you have to tell me that was so important? Or was that it?"

"No, that wasn't it, but I'm glad we are on the same page now."

"So is it about your sister? Who I know is a Sister, capital S?"

My cheeks turn cold. "What? No. It was the amulet, remember?"

Her hand moves to my face and holds my chin as if I'm a little kid. "Drake, being a Knowing doesn't mean you actually *know* much about the Craft. Your story was smart, but my mother knows history.

Our history. There's no such thing as an amulet that stores magical energy—not that much energy. I know Mona is a Sister. But what intrigues me is this: how come her energy comes and goes?"

She stares at me for a while, her gaze switching back and forth between my eyes, but I can't make myself tell her. She releases my chin and fishes a cigarette out of her small pink purse. "Mind if I light up?"

I snap out of my stupor. Until a while ago, smoking gave me chills because of the whole fire incident. Now I know it wasn't my fault, but old habits die hard. "Let's go outside."

On the deck, she gives the cigarette small puffs. For some reason, I'm reminded of Jane. Maybe because I don't know many smokers.

"So?" she asks.

"It's complicated," I say.

She sighs, then takes a deep puff and blows the smoke in my face.

It smells of tobacco, cloves, and, strangely, sweet fruit. I cough a little. "That wasn't very nice."

"You need it to clear your head," she says. "Now, let me ask again: is Mona a witch?"

"Y-yes."

She blows another cloud of smoke in my direction. "Is she the Singularity?"

My eyes water a little. I was trying to come up with a story for this meeting, but it's silly to lie to Yara if I'm going to ask for her help. I'm compelled to tell her the truth. "Yes."

Yara's eyes bulge, but she says nothing. She recovers soon, though. She sighs and asks in a dreamy tone, "Why can't you be my knight in shining armor?"

"I'm already someone else's knight."

"Did you fall for Skye?"

"What? What does that have to do with anything?"

"Please, just answer me," she says in a soft voice.

"Yes." I'm used to the cigarette smell by now.

"Do you *love* her?"

"Yes. I love Skye," I say.

Wait! Why did I say that? Most importantly, why did I say it to Yara, and not to Skye?

She nods in slow motion. "Why did you ask me here today, Drake?"

Being direct is the best course of action now. "We need to cure Boulder. I need you to help Mona save him."

"How?"

I try to remember the witch-speak. "Mona has plenty of magical energy, but she doesn't know the healing rituals. You need to guide her."

"Can't you ask Skye?"

I shake my head. "I did. She doesn't want to. She says it's too risky. That it may reveal Mona's powers."

Yara bites her lip and puts out the cigarette in a deliberate motion. "She's right, you know?"

Despair comes over me, and I grab her hands. "Yara, please. I've told you a secret that puts my sister in danger. I'm trusting you. Please help me. Please help my friend."

Her eyes search my face. "Don't worry. Your secret is safe with me. And I will help you."

***

"You told her?" Mona is not amused.

"She already knew, Mona. Yara got it the moment you showed

downstairs the other day. Regular witches can't turn it on and off."

"This is the worst-kept secret in history," she growls. "Do you trust her?"

I open my arms. "I don't really have a choice, but I trust her. I met her best friend after, and she didn't have a clue. And those girls share *everything*."

"I have to talk to Pain about it," Mona says.

"Are you in?"

"I have to talk to Pain, Drake."

"Okay. But I don't understand why."

"It's just…I want to do it, Drake. Boulder is all right. Even if he weren't, I have a duty to help. We're doing the right thing. But I need to know the consequences."

"And Pain?"

"She helps me think. And she's a part of this now too."

"Pain? How so?"

Mona looks at me in disbelief. "For the same reason why you're doing this for Boulder."

"Oh," I say, "I get it."

"Besides, she almost got killed on the day of the earthquake. She's part of this mess. And Drake?"

"What?"

"The story you told me about Jane. When she came here?"

Mona didn't look well when I gave her the highlights of my nightmare meeting with Jane. "Yes?"

"Do you believe her?"

I do, but I don't want Mona trusting Jane. I may be wrong.

"I don't know, Mona."

Chapter 39: Skye

Drake and I have barely spoken since we parted ways bitterly three days ago. I called him a couple of times, but he would only utter monosyllables. It's better that way for now. We need to rethink some things in our relationship. At least, I know I do.

Pain's words from our conversation from yesterday still resonate with me. I've been thinking about my feelings for Drake and about our less-than-stellar few days.

I push it all out of my mind, though. My head needs to be clear for today.

This is it. The dreaded deposition I have to give. Connor asked Aunt Gemma if we could use the house. It's going to be a long day.

I'm glad Drake didn't mind. He trusts me. Drake even seemed eager for me to spend the day with Connor. Maybe I'm imagining things.

Connor brought a Sister with him—a witness. Her name is Vanessa. I wonder if they're dating, but I don't see any flirting between them. Well, not more than the usual.

She's also a stenographer. She will write down everything I say. As if the AV equipment weren't enough.

While she sets it up, he says, "All right. Remember, Skye, this is just a formality. You will basically say to the camera all that you told me about Brianna. But the keyword here is 'formal.' We'll follow the procedures and the language. Is that all right with you?" After I nod, he adds, "I'm sorry about the potion, but it's mandatory."

I'm amused by this display of concern from Connor. He seems to care for me now. Where was this thoughtful Connor two years ago when we were dating?

Vanessa preps the Truth potion. She smiles at me and asks, "Are you comfortable?"

"Yes," I say.

"Good. We'll be here a while. I brought you a pitcher of water, a glass, and some biscuits." She points to the coffee table. "Do you need to use the restroom?"

I tell her I don't. She's so perky. With her gold locks and constant smile, it's as if the sun is shining upon her all the time.

She adjusts the tripod-mounted tiny camera and tells Connor, "We're ready."

He sits across from me, off-camera. "Let's do it."

Vanessa starts recording.

Connor narrates. "This is Connor Wallace, member of the London coven and temporary supervisor for the Search, Pacific Northwest." He recites the date and time. "I'll conduct the exit interview with Skye Lexington-Ellis, also a London coven Sister, regarding her participation in the Search. This is the official record for the archives, to be complemented later, if necessary."

What does he mean, "if necessary?" I thought we would have Elsa, the Mother with Truth Charm, interviewing me later anyway. Does that mean I might be off the hook? I have the Dispel working. I can beat today's interview.

He continues. "Assisting me with equipment and transcribing the

216

session is Vanessa Walker, Sister of Eugene, Oregon, currently residing in Seattle, Washington. Miss Walker will be administering the Truth potion." He nods to her.

She gets the syringe from the tray and approaches me, entering the frame. She kneels down, preps my arm, and injects the potion into it.

I hope Yara's Dispel holds. It should. If it could resist that night with Miranda, it certainly will help me today.

"Let's give it a few moments to make sure the potion is active. Miss Lexington-Ellis, may I call you Skye during the course of this interview?"

I nod.

He motions to his throat and mouths, "Speak up."

"Yes." I feel like a hostile witness in one of those courtroom movies.

"Skye, please tell us how you got involved with the Search."

It's odd seeing Connor act all business-like. He has command of the situation. He sounds older. Maybe he has really changed.

"Skye?"

"Oh, of course. I was asked by the London Mothers to move to Seattle and help with the Search. I was assigned to Greenwood High School. Gemma Rowland, a trusted Knowing, is my host in Seattle."

"Any particular reason for your selection?"

"At the time, I was told my True Sight Charm would be a valuable asset to identify the Singularity. Later, you—I mean, Connor Wallace—informed me Greenwood was the most probable neighborhood for the Singularity Daybreak."

Connor grins and nods his approval.

"Give us an account, in your own words, of your progress since you arrived at Greenwood."

I try to arrange the facts in my head. Almost everything will be the truth anyway. I only have to fudge the Singularity's real identity and some facts about the school fire. Feeling relaxed, I begin. "I assumed I would be the only Sister at school, but I was surprised to sense another Sister there. I learned her name was Jane Kaplan, a rogue Sister, and possibly a member of a Night coven."

This is not hard. I have no idea of telling if the Dispel is working or not, but I trust Yara's skills. I have no option. And the prospect of having the examinations end today make me determined to get this right.

Connor motions to me to go on.

"Jane Kaplan was openly hostile to me at first, and I—"

I yelp. All of a sudden, a massive wall of energy hits me. It's like I've been knocked down by a sea wave. Connor feels it too and lets out a grunt. Vanessa takes a step back.

Green light surrounds us. Our ears ring with a sound reminiscent of crystal glasses clinking.

No, Goddess, no.

Connor recovers fast. "That's the girl. Brianna has awoken." He stands up and gets his phone. "Calling the hospital," he tells me. "Vanessa, call London."

It's the Singularity, all right. Not Brianna, as he thinks. With the energy all around us, I hope Connor cannot tell the direction of the energy. I know I can. My True Sight tells me the source was located west of the hospital.

While they dial, I run to my room. I left my phone there.

I call Drake. When he answers, I blurt out, "What have you done?"

Chapter 40: Drake

Today is the day. Skye will be busy with her interview. She won't be able to drop by or call.

The three girls who will be trying to help Boulder are meeting with me at my house before we go to his. Yara, Mona, and Pain look at me with expectant eyes. I'm the director, the coach, the leader. It's *my* best friend's life after all.

"Before we go," I say, "I want to make sure we're all a hundred percent in."

"I'm with Mona," Pain declares as soon as the words leave my mouth.

"I'm with you." Yara points to me.

"And I'm with Mona as well. So it's your decision, sis."

Mona nods. "Let's do it, Drake. I mean, that's the whole point of having this…" She sweeps her arms around. "…power, right? It makes no sense having it and not using when someone needs it."

A sudden urge compels me to step forward and hug Mona. "Even if it doesn't work, I'm so proud of you, sis. And thankful."

"Come on, Drake. You're embarrassing me." Despite her words, her face lights up.

We ride there in my loyal Volvo. I'm a little late on purpose. I hope Sean has already gone home by the time we arrive. I know today is Priscilla's day off too.

"This piece of junk is making a loud noise," Mona says from the back seat.

"I know. It's the engine. I think."

"I'm joking. Come on, Drake, relax a bit. Look at your hands," she replies.

I'm grabbing the wheel so hard my knuckles are white.

Yara pats my hands. "Don't worry, D. We've been rehearsing the ritual at home. Without energy. Mona knows what to expect."

Mona says, "She walked me through it many times. It'll be all right."

I look at her in the rearview mirror. "Just don't release too much energy, Mona. This is already too risky. Stay inside your limits. Yara, let her know if her energy goes off the charts. If it's too much, it'll alert the witches nearby."

Yara snorts. "Not that many witches around, silly."

"They have at least some witches a few blocks from there," I remind them. "Taking care of Brianna at Seattle General."

"That's like ten blocks away," Pain says.

"Either way, it's too close for my taste," I point out.

We ride in silence. Pain makes everyone check their cells. If needed, we'll be exchanging texts. Pain is our lookout.

"I wish Greta were coming too," Yara says. "More energy for the commune."

Mona says, "Believe me, I've got all the energy we need. Besides, we don't want to share my secret with more people."

I park half a block down from Boulder's house. Paranoia is at an all-time high today.

We walk to the house. I go first with Yara. The street is calm. As always, clouds hide the sun. I look down. Someone cleaned the driveway; it doesn't have Boulder's bloodstains anymore.

"Yara, do you sense anyone?"

"No. No Sisters around."

"Let me know, all right? If there's a risk of them identifying Mona, we'll abort on the spot."

Looking back, I wave to Pain and Mona. They join us. I ring the doorbell.

Mona is biting her lip. Pain squeezes her hand and smiles at her. "It will be all right." Mona leans her head against Pain's shoulder.

"Hey, a crowd today," Serena says. This is her shift. She's the nurse taking care of Boulder.

The living room is so different from the day of the party. No one would imagine that it was once filled with music and laughter. My guests enter and gather around the sofa while I talk to Serena.

"Hey, Serena."

She smiles. "Hey, Drake. Is it your shift?"

"Yeah. I brought my sister and her friends today. We're doing a circle of prayer for Boulder." It's not technically a lie.

"Oh, sweetie. I don't know. It's only two at a time, you know that."

I make puppy eyes at her. "I know, I told them that. What if it's only three of us? It'll mean a lot. Boulder needs all the help he can get."

Serena wears a tiny golden cross in a pendant over her nurse uniform. She rubs it for a second. She whispers to me, "Okay. But don't let anyone else know."

"Thanks. You're an angel, Serena."

"No, I'm not." Serena glances at the three girls and does a

double-take. "Those are some pretty girls, Drake," she says in a playful voice. "Does your girlfriend know about what you've been doing?"

Oh, Serena, did you have to bring that up? No, Skye doesn't know and doesn't approve. In fact, she would be pretty mad if she found out.

I just smile at her and mumble, "Thanks. The short one is my sister, by the way."

But my nurse friend has already destabilized me. I had managed to bury the thought, at least for a while. Now I feel sneaky. Why? Why do I feel that way? I'm doing the right thing.

I hope.

Jeff shows up and gives me a handshake. "Sean just left," he says. "I really appreciate you boys keeping my son company."

I force a smile. "I know, Jeff. You tell me every day."

"It's worth repeating."

"Hey, my friends and I want to do a prayer. Non-denominational. Do you have any objections—"

He holds his hand up. "Of course not. Every bit helps. I'll be upstairs with Diana. She's having one of her bad days."

I nod. Boulder's mother's health has gone downhill, and Jeff mentioned strong antidepressants. Jeff walks up the stairs, running his fingers through his gray hair.

Serena introduces herself to my gang and goes to the room Boulder is living in now. His parents converted the large den into a patient's room. They couldn't take all the bulky equipment upstairs.

The smiley nurse comes back and points to her watch. It's time. Yara stands up and joins Mona and me. Serena waves us in.

When I open the door to Boulder's room, Yara gasps. She hasn't seen him since the day after the accident, when Boulder was in pretty bad shape, but still looked like Boulder.

Now he is pale, his pasty face devoid of emotion. His muscles are losing their tone. The skull in his Gears of War tat looks like an ominous sign now. His breathing is forced, unnatural. He looks smaller than ever. Yara squeezes my hand.

"It's okay," I say. "That's why we're here today."

She nods and lets go of my hand.

This has been his room for a while. No computer, no futons, no Sean and I laughing.

I turn to Boulder. "Hey, big man. New visitors today. I think you'll enjoy this afternoon."

Yara approaches the bed, leans over him, and kisses his forehead. She whispers something into his ear.

Mona stares at Boulder, but doesn't say anything. A benign smile forms on her lips. "We're doing a good thing here."

I nod and look at my cell. If an unexpected visitor shows up, Pain will text me right away.

They installed a door with a small glass window, so the family, Serena, and the other shift nurses can check the room without going in all the time. I wish I could lock the door, but it has no lock. "Let's do this," I say.

Yara leads Mona to one side of the bed and moves to the opposite one. "No worries, Mona. Just like we practiced, right?"

"Right," Mona says, her voice faltering a bit.

Yara opens her purse, gets out a handful of bottles, and pushes them into Mona's hands. Yara opens the first one, some kind of clear ointment, and spreads a thin layer of it on Boulder's head.

She gives the bottle back to Mona, who hands her the second one right away. They seem to have practiced this part too.

Yara tells me while moving to the next bottle, "Since we don't have a bonfire, and we can't use the smoke of offerings, I'm making do with alternatives."

They work fast. Yara takes a deep breath and announces, "We're ready."

Standing by the door, I take one last look through the glass window and nod.

The two girls hold hands above Boulder's head. Yara chants in a low voice. My sister soon closes her eyes and joins her.

Their hand grip is similar to the one trapeze artists use: they grab each other's wrists. They must have agreed on a signal, because from time to time, I see one of Yara's fingers tapping my sister's forearm while holding the grip. Mona tenses up every time this happens, and soon after Yara's arms tremble, as she just have received a jolt of energy.

My gaze switches from them to Boulder, to my watch, to the cell, and to the living room through the door's window. In one of these passes, I see Serena approaching our room.

She stops and stands right before the door. She looks past me, at the two girls beside Boulder.

I turn to the bed. The girls have their eyes closed, hands held together, and are murmuring something. I look back at the door.

Serena nods and smiles. Then she winks at me and goes away.

I take a deep breath.

"Keep going, Mona," Yara whispers. "Drake, we're not getting results. We'll try a little more."

"Okay," I whisper back, trying not to disrupt their ritual.

A couple of minutes after that, Yara's brow furrows. She taps

Mona's forearm. Then she taps again, more insistently.

"Mona, slow down," Yara's voice is low but her tone is urgent.

Yara's torso jerks a bit.

"Mona," Yara says in her normal voice. "This is too much." She still holds Mona's arms with resolute strength.

"I can control it," Mona says in a quiet voice.

"That's not it," I say. "They might sense you."

"There's no one close. Now, quiet, please," Mona murmurs.

Yara opens her eyes to look at me. "She's the one directing the energy now."

Mona ignores us.

Yara's body jerks back again. "Goddess, Mona, release it slowly."

"I know." I hear distress in Mona's voice.

"Mona," I say. "Take it easy."

She nods.

Right after that, Yara gasps. She's pushed back as if someone punched her. "Stop," Yara says, almost out of breath.

This time Mona shakes her head.

"Let go of me," Yara says. "It's over."

"Can't…break the circle," Mona says, her teeth clenched. "You told me."

Yara's hands open and she tries to twist her arms out of my sister's grasp. Mona holds on, her fingers digging into the flesh of Yara's forearms. Yara groans when another energy wave hits.

Mona starts to shake.

"Mona!' I say. "Let go!" I approach and try to separate the two, but it's as if a powerful magnetic force keeps them together. I don't feel the energy, but Mona's shaking harder.

"He needs me! We need to help him."

Then I see it out of the corner of my eye. His finger moves.

Boulder is awake!

His hand slowly turns. I let go of Yara and grab his hand. He squeezes my fingers in a weak grip.

"Boulder is moving! We did it!" I don't care who hears me.

Boulder's eyelids tremble a bit and soon they open.

I instinctively look at the door. Serena's staring back at us, frowning.

"You did it, Mona. He responded," I say. "You can stop now."

But Mona is vibrating like mad. Her eyes are forced shut, her teeth gritted, her face a mask of pain. "I can't…control," she growls.

Yara is terrified and still cannot escape Mona's grip. She lets out a cry.

Mona and Yara scream. A wave of green light washes over all of us with a whooshing sound. Yara is thrown across the room. My sister takes two steps back and hits the wall right behind her.

Serena opens the door. She, Boulder, and I are only hit by the sound and light. A loud clinking noise takes over the room. We stay frozen in place.

The green light slowly vanishes. The jingling sound hangs in the air, joining the beeping noise of one of the machines.

Boulder is blinking. Mona is gasping for air, plastered to the wall.

Yara gasps. "Goddess, Mona!" She is holding onto her back as if in pain. Her lips are bleeding, but she looks fine otherwise.

Boulder gapes at me. He has no expression and doesn't say anything. But he's awake. That's all that matters.

Serena rushes to the bed and finds her patient awake. She's taken aback, but soon her nurse training kicks in. She takes his pulse while snarling at me, "You have a lot to explain, mister. What was that?"

She's not an angel anymore.

My cell vibrates.

Only it's not Pain.

"What have you done?" Skye asks in a cold voice.

***

"What have you done?" Skye repeats.

"Where are you?" I ask.

"Are you with Mona?"

"Why?"

"What did you do? Did you try to save Boulder?"

"Skye—"

"Drake, I saw the wave. I felt it. All the Sisters felt it. All of them!"

"She's with me."

"Run away. Now!"

"Where?"

"Anywhere but there! They'll be after you. They might find you. Don't let them get Mona."

I hear a loud noise on the phone. Skye hangs up.

Boulder's father is at the door, agape, looking at me and at Boulder in turns.

Diana appears behind him, crying wildly. "My little boy," she says, while running to the bed.

Boulder's eyes move from Jeff to Diana.

Jeff grabs me by the shoulder. "What happened? What did you do? We saw a green light—"

I hold his arms. "Jeff, listen to me. Boulder will get better. This is real. But you cannot tell anyone about this."

"It's a miracle," Jeff whispers.

"Jeff! Please. Listen to me. You saw nothing. No one came here. Do you understand? This is important. These girls will be in trouble if you say anything. Not police trouble. Death trouble." I look into his eyes, as if trying to drill the message into his brain.

"Why?"

"It doesn't matter! Just promise me that you, Diana, and Serena will never tell anyone. Never. Please."

Jeff grabs my arm. "Of course. We won't tell."

"Thanks. Now I have to go."

He goes to the bed to see his son. Diana is hugging Boulder and sobbing.

"Girls, we need to leave. Now!" I say.

"Why?" Yara asks.

"The Sisters are coming."

***

My car doesn't start. When I turn the key, it coughs and sputters, but it doesn't turn over. The next time I try, the only sound it makes is a click.

"What's going on?" Pain asks.

"I don't know. It's not the engine. And it's got gas. Maybe it's the battery."

"What now?"

"Pain, go inside and ask Jeff for a jump start," I say, imagining how I'm going to go back there and bother the guy who just had his son brought back to life.

She leaves in a hurry.

We hear a motorcycle engine.

"Jane!" Mona yelps.

We look at each other.

"Let's go," I say.

We all jump out of the car and run for a block.

"It's a Sister," Yara says, trying to catch her breath. "I can sense her."

I turn to Mona. "Run! Just go! I'll stop her."

Mona runs to the next house's backyard and disappears behind the fence. The bike's roaring engine is closer. Yara and I brace ourselves.

"We need to split," I say.

Yara nods. Before we can set off, we hear a whooshing noise and a loud thud behind us. Someone has just shot at us.

It's getting dark, but I can still see where it came from. A woman riding a bike has a gun trained on us.

I jump in front of Yara, trying to shield her, just as we hear another shot.

A sharp pain traverses through my spine. I scream. My muscles become rigid. I'm still embracing Yara, and my weight is too much for her slight frame. I fall on top of her.

I'm conscious, but I can't move or speak. The pain is now an intense, dull ache spreading over my body. And I can't feel my legs. I can't feel my arms either!

My head is still turned to the street. I can see our attacker.

She accelerates her bike and stops near us. She climbs out of the bike, holsters her pistol, and removes her helmet.

It's not Jane.

She's a tall woman in her thirties with dirty blonde hair and a scrawny face.

"Drake, are you okay?" Yara wheezes under me.

The woman answers for me. "He's paralyzed. I couldn't shoot to kill, could I? Might damage the Singularity."

I can hear them. And I hear another engine over the one from the woman's bike near to me.

"Who are you?" Yara yells at the woman.

The biker woman squats next to us. Her deliberation is unnerving. She is relishing our powerlessness.

"The question is…who are you? You're the Singularity, aren't you? I can sense you now."

Another bike is coming close fast. I see it, coming from behind the skinny witch.

It's Jane.

She's approaching crazy fast, driving with one hand, her helmet in her other hand.

The woman notices it too. She stands up in a flash, trying to get out her pistol, but Jane is already too close. The woman tries to get out of the way. Jane brakes, and her bike skids and slows down. She swings her arm back and hits the blonde square in the head with the helmet.

A loud thudding sound later, the woman is on the ground. She doesn't move.

Jane keeps the motor running, kicks the stand down, and jumps off the bike. She walks over to us. Just like the crazy woman did. "Where's Mona?" she asks.

Yara says, "She's not here."

"Where is she?" Jane growls while dragging me away from Yara.

"I'm here," my sister says from behind me.

No, no, no. Mona, go away. I make a tremendous effort to move, to talk, but nothing happens.

"Is Drake okay?" Mona's voice trembles.

"He's paralyzed," Jane says. "It'll go away soon. She shot him with a potion." She shows me a dart with an empty small flask. "Girl, drag him away from here. Hide him and run. Your energy will attract Sisters nearby. I sensed two of them already on my way here. Mona, let's go."

"What? I... I don't know," Mona mumbles.

Jane's voice is stern. "Trust me. I'm your best chance. Stay here, and the Night sisters will get you. Or the other kind. Either way, your life is over." She pauses and adds, "And I need your help too."

"Okay," my sister replies in a timid voice, her eyes huge.

No, Mona! I shouldn't have told you about Jane. You're pitying her. That was Jane's plan! And I fell for it. I just gifted Mona to Jane.

Jane kneels down next to the woman and injects her with a yellow liquid. "Don't worry, Drake. It's Forget. Told you I wouldn't kill anyone. This is Scythe, a witch assassin. The one who stabbed me."

Then Jane approaches me and does something behind my back. Neither Yara nor Mona protest.

Yara drags me away. I want to scream. Don't let my sister go.

It's no use. Yara leaves me behind the bushes separating two houses. "Sorry, Drake. I wish I had brought a Dispel."

She kisses me on the lips and runs away.

And I watch in horror as Mona climbs onto Jane's bike and they disappear into the night.

Chapter 41: Skye

Connor bangs on my locked door. "Skye! Open it!"

I hang up on Drake and take a deep breath. My mind needs to be sharp. I open the door.

Connor barges in. "Did you feel the wave?"

"Of course!"

"I mean, where did it come from?"

I have a split-second to decide. I need to gamble. "From the general direction of the hospital."

Connor lets out a loud gasp. "Are you sure? Think hard. Really hard."

"What are you talking about?"

He steps closer. "It's not Brianna! The Sisters at the hospital might not have True Sight, but they're close to Brianna's room. They can tell the wave didn't come from there. Where is the Singularity, Skye?"

I'm afraid he might hit me, but he doesn't threaten me in any way. It helps me to keep my voice down. "I don't understand, Connor. Brianna is the one."

Vanessa pops her head in. She holds a cell to her ear. Her voice is tense when she talks to us, "They are saying the source is Greenwood, but not the hospital. One of ours recognized a Night

Sister leaving her post near the hospital and moving west. We've sent two Sisters over there as scouts."

Connor tells her, "Okay. Keep me posted."

Vanessa goes downstairs.

"So? Explain this to me."

"Do you think there might be a second Singularity?"

He scoffs. "Of course there isn't!"

"How do we know? Maybe this is a new one. I mean, it's possible."

His face darkens. His eyes narrow. "Skye, what are you hiding?"

"Nothing."

He becomes strangely calm. Despite his anger, he sits down on the worn-out love seat in my room. He glares at me. "There's only one Singularity, and you know it. Suppose there are two; what are the odds of the second one surfacing in the same town? You know that. And you lied to me. Your True Sight can pinpoint the direction, maybe even the distance, right? My parents study these things. Remember? Only you couldn't have lied, because right now you're under a Truth potion." He leans forward. "Or are you?"

I try to hold his stare, but my lips tremble.

"If you somehow tried to neutralize the Truth potion, it means you intended to lie. In your official interview. Which tells me that you've been lying all along. So Skye, potion or not, this is the time to level with me. Who is the Singularity?"

I shake my head.

He looks at the floor. "Skye. You're throwing your life away."

Chapter 42: Drake

Yara left me in a weird position: on the side path between two houses, behind the bushes. At least I'm hidden from the street. My head is still facing the driveway, though. I see Scythe waking up, clearly lost. She looks around and frowns. Her hand goes to where Jane hit her and comes back with a little blood. She looks at her cell and shakes her head. At last, she climbs on her bike and rides away. Good. One less problem.

Movement comes first to my numb fingertips. It's like coming out of anesthesia after dental work. Soon, I can wiggle my toes. Then my hand responds. Next, my arms and legs. It takes me a while to roll around to a more comfortable position and to regain control of my muscles.

I hate witch stuff.

I need to find Mona right away. Jane might disappear with her for good. Or worse.

Something pokes me near my butt. I reach into my pocket. A cell phone, not mine. Looks like a toy.

Is that what Jane planted in my pocket before leaving? Why would she do that?

I sit on the gravel path and flip open the cell. Its battery is full, and it has a single number in the memory. I dial it.

"Yeah?"

"Jane?"

"Drake, did you leave the area already?" Her voice is muffled by the motorcycle's noise.

"No. Where's Mona?"

"With me. Can't talk now. Leave this place. Remember where we kissed?"

"What?"

"Meet us there at nine. Don't tell anyone. Make sure you're not followed."

Jane hangs up.

She said, "Meet *us*." Mona will be there. Or Jane wants me to believe that.

I need to leave. I test my legs, and they hold up. I wobble between the two houses to the backyard. It's dark. I awkwardly climb the fence to the other side and come out a side street.

The traffic looks normal, but then I notice some cars going way too slow. The drivers are looking at the people on the sidewalks. Looking for Mona.

Just remain calm, Drake. You're not a witch. They can't tell.

I go a couple of blocks east, then turn left. I'll circle around to go back to Jeff's. I need my car. I find it where I left it. When I get close, I see Pain inside. She's looking at the road. I knock on the window, startling her.

She opens the driver's door for me, and I climb inside.

"Where's Mona?" she asks with an anxious voice, her hand grabbing my jacket.

"Jane has her. But I think it's okay."

"What?" Pain shakes me. "How is this okay?"

"Pain, get a hold of yourself. Jane has her, but she told me to meet them tonight. Mona is safe." I could add that we cannot do anything about it anyway, but I don't. "Now, is the car working?"

She lets go of my jacket. "Yes. Boulder's father gave me the charger," she says, pointing to an orange Black & Decker jump-starter on the backseat. "I left the car running for a while."

Praying silently, I turn the key. The Volvo sputters, but this time, the engine turns over.

"Drake, how can you be sure Jane won't harm Mona?"

"I just know," I lie. "I'm positive. Come on, we need to leave. I'll drop you off and call you as soon as I get her back, okay?"

**

The news announcer says nobody knows the source of the green light. City officials have discarded the possibility of terrorism, but will investigate the matter. Greenwood residents are interviewed on TV, saying they thought a radioactive leak had occurred. The TV shows a quick clip of videos uploaded to YouTube, but there's nothing more than a flash of green light. The clinking sound isn't as loud as I experienced it. The witches must be concerned about the Veil. I hope the covens are as influential as they say they are and make this go away soon.

I call Yara.

"Drake!" She sounds relieved. "Are you okay?"

"Yes. You?"

"Got home okay. Nobody stopped me or anything. And Mona?"

"Picking her up in a few."

"What's going on?"

"I'll let you know when I know. Let's meet and talk tomorrow, okay?"

"Sure. I get it."

"And Yara? Thank you. Really."

"My pleasure, *gatinho*."

I don't know Portuguese, but I'm pretty sure what she means.

When I'm about to leave to meet Jane, Sean calls.

"Dude! Where are you? Have you heard?"

"That Boulder woke up?"

"Yes! Come on, man! Why aren't you shouting?"

"I am. Inside. I truly am."

"They're doing some tests. Boulder's responding. It's too early to say, but it's looking up. A long recovery period, but he'll come through. We'll be the three Musketeers again, huh?"

"Awesome, Sean!" I'm so glad that this mess I put everybody through at least served its purpose.

"So do you want to hang out? We need to celebrate. No beer, though. My vow is strong. Only sodas for me now."

"I need to pick up my sister."

"Always the boy scout, huh? Okay, but stop by tomorrow. Let's go see Boulder together."

"Sure thing, Sean. I gotta go now."

***

I hang up. The only time Jane and I kissed was when she slipped me a Fancy Me potion. We were close to Priscilla's house. The dark road is a great secluded place, actually. I drive there.

My destination is not far from my house, but it feels like it takes forever to get there. What if I'm kidding myself? What if this is just another one of Jane's elaborate plans?

Right after I pass Priscilla's house, I see three silhouettes: a motorcycle and two people.

My heart beats fast; my hands sweat. Those two seconds between seeing the dark shapes and identifying them are the most anxiety-ridden of my life.

But Jane comes through. Mona is right by her side.

I stop the car in front of them and get out. The squeezing hug Mona gives me makes it all right.

"Jane needs to talk to you," my sister says. "I'll wait in the car."

I give Mona my cell. "Call Pain. She's dying to talk to you."

Jane and I walk a few steps away from our rides. I try not to look at her scarred face. She would resent me for staring.

"I told you to trust me," Jane says.

I'm so happy to have Mona back that I can't resist a little joke. "Well, you have a bit of a reputation."

"Drake!"

"I'm kidding. Thank you, Jane. I mean it. To me, this makes up for everything in the past."

"It's no big deal. I told you."

"Why didn't you keep Mona? You two together could've gone ahead and tried to save him."

"Something tells me that I'm better off handing Mona over to you," Jane says.

"Your Intuition Charm?"

"Maybe. But for practical reasons too. I release magical energy. Sooner or later, I'd attract the Night Sisters, and they would find Mona. Besides, I don't need only Mona to find Jason. I need Skye too."

"Good luck with that. She's pissed at me and won't return my calls."

"Really?" A pause. "Well, at least she will not draw attention to

Mona. Not having a Sister visiting your house is a big advantage now. If she comes back, keep her away from Mona. Use *only* the burner phone I gave you to call me. You have to decide what you're going to do. The covens are closing in; they'll find out who Mona is. We need to move fast."

"Or Mona and I could run," I offer.

"They'll monitor anyone close to Skye and the other Sisters. If you run, everybody will know Mona is the one."

"Or if Brianna tells them."

Jane raises her eyebrows. "See? We should have killed her when we had the chance."

"I thought you wouldn't murder anyone else."

"I said, 'if I didn't have to,' remember? And I don't think I do. I just saved your sister and brought her back to you. Can you do the same for my brother?"

"I will."

"Promise?" Her stare burns into my eyes.

I gaze right back at her damaged face. "I promise, Jane."

Chapter 43: Skye

On our way to the airport, Connor looks at me, alert, as if I might break out of the town car at any moment.

"What?" I ask.

"How could you have lied to me? To your coven?"

He doesn't need to worry about the Veil. The driver's a Knowing.

"Connor, please."

"Here's what's going to happen now: we'll wake up Brianna even if it kills her. Now that we know she's not the Singularity, we're not so concerned with her well-being anymore. A group of Healing Sisters will be summoned to make a commune ritual to wake her up."

"Why are you telling me this?"

"When Brianna wakes up, she will tell us who the real Singularity is. Why don't you tell me the truth now before we get it from her anyway? It'll lessen the punishment by the covens."

"I'll take my chances."

His scowl almost hides his Allure. "I was so proud of you. I don't understand why you're doing this."

Nothing I say will help my case, so I just look out the window.

"I will still try to help you as much as I can." His voice is not Connor's usual one. It's softer. Caring.

What am I going to do? Wild scenarios run through my head. Run away. Break the Veil. Even ludicrous ones, like asking Yara to brew me a powerful Forget potion, erasing everything from the last few weeks from my memory.

I have no strategy to face a Sister with a Truth Charm.

Mona will be outed, and I'll be the one doing it.

And Drake. What am I going to do about Drake?

***

The British Airways flight is delayed. Connor and I avoid eye contact while we wait in the security line. Sea-Tac airport is not too busy tonight.

A familiar voice calls my name. "Skye!"

Drake waves to me. He has just turned the corner close to the check-in desks. He is walking fast while motioning to me to get out of the line.

Connor says, "I can't allow you to—"

"Connor, don't even start. I'll talk to him, and you can go to hell."

I step out of the security line. Connor follows me begrudgingly. He stays away from me, though.

Drake meets me near a Starbucks. I lead him to two isolated chairs so we can have some privacy.

"Are you all right? What's going on?" he asks. "You didn't return my calls. When Aunt Gemma finally picked up the phone, she told me you were going to England. With him." He points to Connor.

"Drake, you don't understand. They don't know about Mona, but they know I lied. I'm being shipped back to London to face the Mothers."

He's ashen. "They don't believe it's Brianna anymore?"

"The energy was so intense that they could tell the direction of the source. That's why they sent Sisters to Boulder's neighborhood."

"Skye, I had no idea—"

"Listen. They will be monitoring everyone I talked to in Seattle. Like staking out, following, electronic surveillance, you name it. I can't use a phone. Neither can you. Don't talk to anyone on the phone. Even Mona and Pain must be careful."

Drake shifts about, agitated. "And you're just leaving?"

"I don't have a choice. My coven summoned me."

He makes a dismissive gesture. "To hell with them. You're not beholden to them."

"Actually, I am. Drake, I betrayed the people who loved me, who raised me. I may be banished from my coven."

"Oh, Skye…" He tries to hug me.

"Don't touch me!" My reaction is spontaneous and surprising even to myself.

He's taken aback. I might as well have slapped him.

"I deserve this," he says.

"Why did you do that? Why did you put Mona in that situation?"

"I couldn't live with the thought that I could've done something and chose not to do it. For what it's worth, Mona did everything right, but she lost control at the end." He gazes at his feet. "We saved him, by the way."

"I'm happy for him. I really am. But now everything else is ruined. Mona is in danger again. Now I have to go. Do you know what you've done? All we did, all the lies, were for nothing. I deceived my friends, my Sisters, my mother, my coven. I was tortured. Jane almost killed me. And, in the end, it was all for nothing. You exposed Mona. Your own sister. *You* ruined it."

Drake looks at me again. His face is all tensed up, but he tries to keep his voice steady. "I see that. I'm truly sorry. Please understand that I needed to do it. Mona felt the same way. She knew the risks to herself, but neither of us though it would harm you."

"Now everybody, including the Night covens, will eventually know about Mona. Who she is, where she lives. The Veil might be broken. It almost was, with the green light and everything. It's only a matter of time before they figure out it's Mona. Our only hope is that they're looking for someone who is about seventeen. But once they put it together like we did, she's done for."

He takes a deep breath and straightens his back. "Let's fix this. What can I do?"

"You can't do anything. Now I can't do anything either." My voice sounds weak.

"Let me help you, Skye. I put you in this situation."

"It's funny. You took pity on Jane because she was shunned. Now I may end up just like her. A rogue Sister. No one will ever teach me again, Drake. That's it for me."

His eyes go wide. "No. Don't think like that. We can fix it. We can figure it out, Skye. It's not the end of the world."

"It is to me! It's who I am. It's *all* I am."

"But Skye, you're so much more."

This throws me off. I look down. My hands can't stop fidgeting.

He puts his hand over mine. "I'm just saying we can beat this. The two of us, together."

I shake my head. "We already tried that, Drake. Look where it got us. Look where it got Mona. I feel for her. I'll pray to the Goddess for her. I hope she turns out okay. Involving Mona is my only regret. Keep an eye on her; drive her everywhere."

"What about *us*, Skye?" He tries to hide it, but his voice quivers.

I remove my hand from his and look into his eyes. "I made a

mistake. I'm not coming back." My chest tightens, but I need to do it. It's how I feel. "It's over, Drake. We're over."

He stares at me in disbelief.

I stand up and move to get back to the line.

But Drake comes after me and blocks my path. "Wait, Skye." He stares into my eyes. He's breathing hard, but his tone is composed. "Let's figure out *us* later. Right now, just tell me what I can do to help."

"You've done enough," I say. "You betrayed me, Drake."

I turn fast and leave. When I'm about to go around the corner, an overwhelming feeling takes over me. I stop and take one last look at Drake.

After that moment of weakness, I'm gone.

Chapter 44: Drake

If romantic comedies taught me anything, it is that rushing to the airport at the last minute to plead with a girl always leads to a happily ever after.

I botched it.

I walk through the airport, devastated. Somehow, I find my way back to the parking garage. I arrive at the car, having no idea how I got there. Mona is waiting for me. We get in, and I drive in silence.

When we're on the I-5, she says, "It didn't go well, did it?"

"No."

"When is she coming back?"

"She isn't." I can barely hear myself. I sneak a peek at Mona.

She covers her mouth with her hand. "Do you want to talk about it?"

"Not right now."

She looks out of the window. "Do you want to talk about something else?"

"Please. Anything."

"I spent a few enlightening hours with Jane," she says with a hesitant voice. "She told me Jason's story. And hers. In detail."

"Do you trust her, Mona?"

"Do you?"

"She's a master manipulator. Or was. I don't know anymore. I'm sure her story is true, but it may also be part of a long con of hers."

"She didn't harm me. I want to help her, Drake."

"Really? What good came from helping Boulder?"

Mona puts her hand on my shoulder. "He'll survive, won't he? What else matters?"

"That's a good point. Let's help Jane then. Why not? But who's helping you?"

She squeezes my shoulder in a tender gesture. "Well, you. And who knows? Maybe someone is watching over us, Drake. We're still here. Maybe we can get out of this jam."

I nod, but my thoughts are still with Skye.

"Come on," Mona says. "Look on the bright side. At least I didn't destroy the city this time."

But I can't make myself chuckle.

Mona slaps the dashboard. "Okay, I need to tell you. I know for a fact that you love Skye."

"How can you know that?"

"I saw your aura with her glasses."

I scoff. "Okay. It's not that big of a revelation, you know?"

"Yeah, but here's the thing: a big red aura shows the person is in love."

"And?"

"And I saw hers too. I never told her, but hers is as red as yours, big bro. Maybe a deeper red, even."

The car leaves the lane for a second. I stare at Mona, who beams at me.

But I can't smile. I feel like someone punched me in the stomach.

***

246

Why is all this happening?

I can't really blame anyone. If I must blame someone, I'd better start with myself.

But I'll fix it. I will fix everything.

The image of Skye leaving is seared in my memory. The beautiful face I know so well was cold. Her lips were curved down. Stray strands of hair fell on her face. The buttoned-up blouse covered half of her neck, as if suffocating her. She looked broken inside.

I remember how Skye stopped and raised her chin. She was about to say something, but she didn't. She gave me one last glimpse, those once loving blue eyes piercing mine. It could be an accusatory gaze or a regretful one. Maybe I'll never know.

It doesn't matter. She stopped and looked back. That meant something.

I'll do everything to help her. I owe her.

And I hope she takes me back. I won't give up. I can't, really.

That girl put a spell on me.

###

AUTHOR'S NOTE

Thank you for reading BROKEN SPELL. Please let your friends know about it! Word-of-mouth is vital for an author. If you enjoyed the book, please leave a review on Amazon and Goodreads, even if it's just a short paragraph. Your review makes a big difference and would be much appreciated.

For updates on the next book in this series and to be the first to hear about new releases, sign up for my author newsletter (http://bit.ly/fabiobuenoemail/). Your email will never be shared, and you can unsubscribe at any time.

I love to hear from readers! Connect with me on my website (FabioBueno.com), Facebook (Facebook.com/FabioBuenoAuthor), Twitter (@_FabioBueno_), or email me at fabio@fabiobueno.com.

All the best,
Fabio

GLOSSARY

Charms: natural magical powers. Each Sister has two, which manifest after Daybreak. Charms are always active and cannot be "turned off" or countered with potions. Most Sisters have an Allure Charm. Other common ones are Athletics, Intellect, Charisma, and Trust.

Coven: a gathering of Sisters. A witch's coven is a second family to her.

Craft: the culture of the witches. It includes their values, traditions, history, and system of beliefs. Magic is but a part of the Craft.

Daybreak: the coming-of-age of a Sister. A Sister's personal magic awakens at Daybreak, around her fifteenth birthday, usually accompanied by a small burst of magical energy.

Goddess: most Sisters believe the Goddess is a deity, but some view the Goddess as a symbol, an icon, or a manifestation of magical energy. Irrespective of belief, all Sisters pray to the Goddess.

Knowing: somebody who knows magic exists, but is not a witch herself.

Magic/Personal Magic/Magical Energy: all living things possess this universal energy, but only witches can tap into it, connect with the Goddess, and create potions and spells.

Night Magic: Night magic, Night coven, and Night Sisters are the twisted versions of the true Craft. Night magic is more powerful than regular magic.

Potions: brewed during rituals and infused with a Sister's personal magic. Require specific ingredients. Popular potions are Fancy Me, Sleep, and Truth. The most common methods of delivery are beverages, oils, serums, and ointments.

Rituals: solo ceremonies performed by Sisters, with the goal of meditation, connecting with the Goddess, and creating spells and potions. A ritual performed by more than one witch is called a commune ritual.

Singularity: the most powerful witch alive. Her reserve of magical energy is exponentially higher than a regular witch's. The Singularity has more than two Charms, and only releases energy when she casts a spell or loses control of her magic.

Spells: prayers and incantations recited during a ritual where the Sister embeds a little of her personal magic into the prayer. Prayers usually require a simple offering to the Goddess and involve burning of herbs, leaves, flowers, oils, or incense.

Talisman/Amulet: a small object imbued with personal magic; a vessel for a spell or potion.

Veil: an unwritten code, followed by all magic users: nobody reveals the existence of magic. It's the Craft's most important rule.

Witch/Sister: a practitioner of the Craft.

Witch Sense: all Sisters release a constant flow of magical energy that can be felt by other Sisters nearby.

ACKNOWLEDGMENTS

Some say that writers live solitary lives, but I believe it's quite the opposite. The wonderful people listed here are responsible for helping BROKEN SPELL spring into existence—and for making its journey to publication 72 times more fun and rewarding.

A huge thank you and big hug to:

My beloved critique group, Writers in The Rain: Brenda Beem, Angela Orlowski-Peart, Suma Subramaniam, Martina Dalton, and Eileen Riccio. True friends and talented authors.

DMs, YA Ninjas, WANAs, and WG2E Street Team: you rock, and you know it.

The super-team: Pixel Artist Martina Dalton designed the cover; Queen Editress Alyssa Linn Palmer and Proofreader Goddess Amanda Shofner edited the novel.

My unofficial mentors: C. C. Mackenzie, Jillian Dodd, Rhonda Hopkins, and Diane Capri.

Beta-readers/alpha-friends: Julie, Claudio, Carlos, Flavia, Jose, and Lucio.

My kids: thank you for your patience and support. You are the light of my life.

Wonder Wife, who inspires me in every way.

ABOUT THE AUTHOR

Fabio resides in the Pacific Northwest with his wife and kids. When not writing or reading, he geeks out with family and friends, solidifies his reputation as the world's slowest runner, and acts very snobbish about movies. He loves to hear from readers and hangs out here:

@_FabioBueno_

Fabiobueno.com

Facebook.com/FabioBuenoAuthor

www.ingramcontent.com/pod-product-compliance
Lightning Source LLC
Chambersburg PA
CBHW070911180626
46817CB00003B/1013